'MY LOVELY WIFE'

BY

Dani Brown

Brought to you from:

With an excerpt from Dani Brown's brand new:
"TOENAILS" pg. 110

~MY DARLING WIFE~

MorbidbookS Is A Grotesque Bizarro Ballet Where The Most Profane Things Occur. An Impious And Perverse Dwelling Of Dark Revulsion. A Cozy Cottage Where Torture Porn And Brutal Bible Tales Are Devised. A Quiet Place To Relax And Spin Tales Of Depravity And Wickedness. A Halfway House For The Disturbed Where Rules No Longer Apply. A Safe Haven For Deviant Serial Killers To Hatch Their Wretched Schemes. Far, Far Off The Reservation. Bring Your Pets. The Tasty Ones Are Always Welcome.

One

Worms and maggots pulse out of the hole in her neck. Big juicy pink night crawlers grow fat with her flesh. I bought them in a shop. The maggots glisten white in the gloom.

She's still alive but barely. The worms and maggots haven't suffocated her. Her chest rises and falls disturbing the flies that have landed on her. Something inside rattles. I might have broken a rib bringing her down here.

My eyes roam up and down her body. She's lost weight. But not enough to see her ribs poking out from beneath her decaying night vest.

Two

I knew I had to have her when I first laid my eyes on her trachea ring. It was a windy day. I nearly walked past her on the street but a sudden gust of wind blew her greying hair off her neck. That was when I saw the hole. Beneath the greying hair she wasn't a plain Jane but a beauty with the most wonderful trachea ring.

I bumped into her accidently on purpose and asked to buy her a cup of coffee to make up for it. With some obvious reluctance she agreed. I can be very persuasive when I need to be. Like when I required her phone number, address and email address (along with her date of birth and mother's maiden name, of course).

I pursued her. I didn't want to frighten her so I wasn't quite relentless. Every time I would pick her up I would give her flowers. A different, more expensive bouquet each time. I'm old fashioned but it worked. Eventually she caved into my advances and agreed to a date.

I took her to the cinema and out for dinner. I paid for everything trying to impress her. I must have because she agreed to a second date. And a third after that. On the third she invited me in. She was innocent and didn't invite me into her bed but she gave me a long deep kiss running her tongue against mine and a glass of red wine before phoning for my taxi.

Three

It wasn't until our fifth date that she let me see her naked. And that was with great reluctance and the lights were dimmed to their lowest setting.

Her grey pubic hairs were properly trimmed like seen on someone younger. I didn't expect that. I thought they would be an untamed jungle. She must have planned ahead. Her creamy breasts were soft with pink nipples staring at the floor. Her armpits and legs were shaved. It seemed all I could do was stare at her and try to see more in the gloom. I hate dimmer switches.

The shadows caught in her cellulite dimples but even they felt smooth when I caressed her thighs. She tried to shrink and push me away but I insisted. I wasn't too forceful, only enough to make her feel wanted.

I led her to the bed and pushed aside the duvet. I wanted her to turn up the light so I could watch her trachea ring without straining my eyes while I pushed in and out of her. But I didn't want to press the issue. It could have frightened her off that first time.

When I stuck my erection in I couldn't tell she had pushed out eight children; although the last one was born nineteen years ago. It felt like I was popping her cherry that late September evening without the messy blood.

The warm inviting hole provided lubricant. I nearly ejaculated upon insertion – it really wasn't what I was expecting. I expected dryness. I thought I might even tear her upon entry without use of Vaseline.

I could tell it hurt her. I could tell by the pained expression on her face and the drops of water in her eyes. She lied and told me that it didn't. She also informed me that she hadn't had any dick since her husband died. She nearly elbowed me in the face reaching for her voice box as I fucked her. I didn't need to know that right that very minute.

I didn't care that she was in obvious pain. I pushed in anyways, slowly, while asking, "Are you okay?" She claimed she was even after tears dripped down her face, whether that was physical pain or emotions, or a bit of both, I never found out. I didn't care that she was in pain and I probably wouldn't have stopped even if she asked me. I was simply pretending to be a gentle caring lover.

I kissed the tip of her nose and eased out. Then I slowly re-entered. I was as gentle as I could be as I wanted to be invited back for more without degrading myself by begging. After a few minutes of gentle thrusting her raised hips in rhythm (it didn't help though, she should have just laid there like a corpse but I didn't tell her this, I didn't want to be thrown out of her bed).

We took it slow. I wanted her to think it was special. That she was special (which of course, due to that trachea ring, she was). I wanted her to think that I loved her and only her. I wanted her to think it was one very magical moment in time where we became one.

I wanted to stick my tongue in her trachea ring then and there but I restrained myself. That would have resulted in me being pushed off her and to the floor for sure. Then she would have chucked my clothes at me and told me to leave.

The tightness and wetness of her was the only reason I reached orgasm that first time. For someone who was married most of most of her adult life, she was very inexperienced. I imagine her late great husband must've looked outside marriage for his pleasure.

I waited and waited for her to achieve orgasm, like a gentleman should. It never happened. Sex was a chore for her. After pumping away for twenty minutes I couldn't take it any longer and blew my infected load inside her tight dark place.

I pulled out and pulled her into my arms. I kissed the top of her greying head and held her as she cried. Her sobs died away and she fell asleep in my arms for the first time.

Even I managed to doze off. I woke up cold in the middle of the night in an empty bed. I wanted to get under the duvet, roll over and go back to sleep but I knew that if I fancied seeing her and her lovely trachea ring again I would have to go looking for her.

Four

I found her in the kitchen doing nothing except staring out the window. I don't know what she was looking at or for. Maybe a sign of her late husband's approval.

I put my arm around her and gently guided her to the table. Her expression was blank making it impossible to tell what she was thinking. I sat across from her and gripped her cold hands with their dry skin in mine. I rubbed the knuckles trying to bring her back to me. Her skin flaked off and snowed on the polished table.

While her stare was distant I examined the trachea ring with my eyes. I was desperate to examine it with my fingers but the time wasn't right. Skin continued to flake from her hands but still she stared through me and through the wall behind.

I don't think she would have noticed if I started prodding her trachea ring but I didn't want to find out and risk losing her. I don't know how long I sat there rubbing her knuckles. It wasn't relevant. I loved her trachea ring. The rest of her would be mine as well even without my love but it was a price I had to pay.

Five

When I asked her to marry me six months later she agreed. I wouldn't have waited so long but I didn't want to scare her.

Being younger and in better health than her I was capable of getting down on one knee. I had taken her on an evening spring walk along the docks. She needed to rest so sat down on the next bench we came across. She didn't know what I had planned. Maybe she would have sat down sooner if she did, or tried to run away.

I left her for a few minutes to get her a drink and ice cream. I looked over my shoulder at her sat there as I walked away. The setting spring sun reflected off her sunglasses radiating her pale flesh. Even without the trachea ring she looked beautiful.

She had curled her hair that evening. The greying locks tumbled over her shoulder in little ringlets. It was held away from her forehead by a series of tiny hair clips with butterflies that glittered in the setting sun.

The wind blew off the river making heavy winter coats a must. But it lifted her curls so they tangled with one another. I watched for at least a minute as her hair was lifted, tangled and re-lifted upon my return.

She didn't notice me standing behind her with two ice cream cones and two bottles of water sticking out of my pockets. The wind was too loud for her impeccable hearing to hear my footsteps coming up behind her.

My hands were too full to lift her greying curls and kiss the back of her neck. I wish I hadn't bought myself an ice cream. Her neck was so tasty. But I risked getting carried away each time I touched it.

I walked to the side of the bench. I'm not sure if she noticed me or not. It was always hard to tell what she noticed and what she didn't, after all, she did raise eight kids. She continued to stare at the river but there was a slight curve of a smile on her thin lips. I don't know if she was smiling due to my return or something that happened in that little world she seemed to occupy all by herself most of the time. I didn't care.

As long as her trachea ring was in the real world, nothing mattered.

I sat next to her and handed her an ice cream cone without saying a word. She took it without looking at me but instead continued staring at the river. Her eyes didn't follow the seagulls or boats. It confirmed my suspicions that she was lost in her own little world.

Her tongue worked that ice cream cone in a way that made me wish it was my dick. She was too prudish for oral sex – a fact I'll be fixing soon. She would always prevent me going down on her. She never gave a reason. I didn't want to risk losing her lovely trachea ring by shoving my cock in her mouth.

But the way she worked that ice cream. Her tongue savoured every lick. I wanted so much for it to do that to my cock. If I stood up and her attention shifted to me she would have noticed my erection. There was no possible way I would have been able to convince her to duck in the public toilets for a quickie so I pulled my heavy winter coat over my lap and watched the boats.

Seagulls fought over bread dropped by tourists. I'm not sure if she noticed or not. It didn't much matter to me. I wanted something else to watch. She wasn't aware of the way she was eating her ice cream and what it implied. The blood left my cock as I finished my mine watching the seagulls.

I took the bottles of water out of my pockets and handed one to her. I chanced a look. She had finished at last. My cock hung limply in my pants disappointed that it wouldn't know the inside of a mouth for several months and then only at force so it wouldn't have that nice tongue lapping.

I reached my hand deeper into my pocket. I thought it had fallen out somewhere when I came out empty handed. The back of my mind told me to stick my hand back in. The tip of my finger brushed against the top of a small box. I plunged my hand in further and gripped it with my fist. It left a pink imprint on my palm.

Twinges of anxiety danced across my chest. It was impossible to know what her answer would be. I might only succeed in making her run off. I wanted so much for her to put the ring on her finger, smile and snap a picture for all her friends on the various social networking sites she belonged to. That was all the answer I needed. That was all the answer I wanted.

I would have to ask soon; she'll want to start walking so she could get home before it was too late and answer the phone if her last born called before his night of drink-induced debauchery. I played with the box in my hand in my pocket. She had no idea.

I slipped off the bench and went down on one knee in front of her staring up at her lovely trachea ring. She must have been able to predict then what I was about to do but she didn't let on.

Whatever world she was in that spring evening wasn't so far removed from the one we share with billions of others. I looked up at her lips to see them curve a little more upwards. I looked up at her eyes – the windows to her soul that were always so guarded, to remember that they were concealed behind sunglasses.

I pulled the box out of my pocket. I lost my voice and couldn't even ask the question. The box sat unopened on my palm. My shaking arm moved over, fingers poised to open but she took it and opened it herself – one of the only times she showed anything even resembling assertiveness. Her neck dropped down as she looked at the ring, obscuring her beautiful trachea ring for a second or so. Her lips turned up further. She took it out and put it on giving me the answer I needed and was so desperate to receive.

Six

I left it to her to plan the wedding. She had already been down the aisle once therefore she had a better idea of how these things worked than I did. I didn't expect the same wedding she had when she was eighteen and walking down the aisle to her childhood sweetheart. I didn't expect her daughters and granddaughters to be dressed in bridesmaid dresses that match their fake tan. I didn't expect a woman of her advanced years to squeeze into a princess gown decorated with LED lights and butterflies, hiding her face behind a veil. She must have been able to read my mind and gave me a wedding I was much more comfortable with.

It wasn't a big church wedding but a nice intimate one at the local registry office with selected friends and family. It was six months after I proposed, in the early winter. We were taking a chance with the weather but I didn't care, I would have been married the next day if she would have allowed it. But she obviously wanted photographs of her second big day, even if they were just taken with her daughter's cheap digital camera.

She wore a lilac trouser suit. The low cut shirt showed off her trachea ring. That was the most beautiful part of her.

She wore a silver chain with a floating heart, a gift from me. It drew attention to the most beautiful part of her.

Her greying locks were once again curled and pulled off her forehead with clips that had butterflies on them – just like the day I proposed. But these were new clips to match her lilac trouser suit. The sky was cloudy, otherwise the sunlight would have reflected off the crystals decorating them.

Not even all her children made it to the wedding, even though they were all very close. I never bothered to learn all their names. My excuse to her was that I was terrible with names. It didn't seem to bother her that much. I know it would have really impressed if I learned but not enough for some decent sex.

I have no children (that I'm aware of) to carry on my name once I die. I don't want any. She's too old to give me any – she made that point clear on our first date. My response made her a bit sceptical. She probably thought I would change my mind. Children complicate things far too much for my liking.

My parents came. Both still alive. Both on their third marriages, like it is some sort of competition between them to see who can destroy the most lives. Their spouses didn't bother showing up. They were invited but it was probably for the best.

Her mother was senile drooling down herself and shitting her pants in an old folks home; her father was long in his grave. I thought it might have been amusing to dig him up and bring him but I didn't say so.

The reception was held at a pub. Just small and local. I'm not into obscene public displays of wealth and false affection and love. She knew that it was the little things that counted. The food was nicer than something big booked somewhere fancy. They put on a nice buffet. Everyone seemed to enjoy themselves.

Seven

She even booked a weekend away in the Lake District for our honeymoon. It was in a posh hotel; each room with an ensuite bathroom and room service. I didn't know how she could afford it but I'm guessing she received a discount of some kind or her children pitched in and paid for it. I didn't object. It was lovely.

Now that she was my wife I tried to go down her again but she pushed me away. I poured some lubricant on her instead before pushing my throbbing cock into her still-tight hole. I wanted to insert it into her mouth.

I tried to go into her a bit faster but she didn't like it. She didn't like me biting her nipple either. It took a lot of effort to blow my infected load (hey, I like to spread around diseases, nothing wrong with that). I wanted to but it would have been easier to cum if I sat on my hands while watching paint dry.

She didn't reach orgasm. She never did. If she let me do new things to her she might find that she enjoys them. I think it is highly likely that she never reached orgasm with her late husband either. I pity the poor man for spending so much of his life with her.

My semen oozed out of her and dripped down her leg when she stood. She wouldn't even let me wipe it off, preferring to shower afterwards by herself, of course. I wanted to lick it but I didn't tell her this.

I sat on the end of the bed playing with my foreskin and sticking my fingers in my mouth to taste her beneath my salted jiz and the chemicals of the lubricant while I waited for her to bathe. I couldn't taste much of her. I couldn't taste much lubricant either. My cum has always had a strong taste of sour milk and salt, like a salty yoghurt.

When she finished she dressed in the large hotel bathroom rather than appear before me wet and wrapped in a fluffy towel. The bright early winter sunlight coming in through the windows probably made her even more bashful than usual.

I continued to eat crust out of my foreskin. She noticed but didn't say anything and left the room. She didn't seem embarrassed by it but it was hard to tell with her. I'm sure she noticed a lot of my more usual habits but never said anything. Because she had only ever been with one man besides myself she might have thought it normal.

I didn't get dressed and follow her. I crawled under the duvet and dreamt of her trachea ring. I dreamt I was inside of it. My entire body, not just my dick. It was weird and vivid. The details have faded now, I wish I had written them down.

Eight

Now she lies on a festering mattress in the fly infested basement. Chained up by both her wrists and ankles. I like the way the chains dig into her flesh. They've rubbed off the skin.

Maggots squirm out from underneath them. I like to think they've been eating away at her.

It took some time to get to this point. Years. Two of them filled with three times a week meaningless boring sex – she couldn't even refuse sex on her period; she didn't get one, she went through the menopause. I thought I had a permanent case of blue balls even though I jerked off daily.

Nine

Then it struck one day. The reason I wanted her so badly was purely down to her trachea ring. I didn't care about her. Only that lovely trachea ring. If I couldn't have her then I would have the trachea ring.

It took months to plan. I wanted her to suffocate while I fuck the tight hole in her throat so I couldn't kill her then do it.

Months of three dull sex sessions a week. But they became more exciting when I thought of my dick pushing in and out of her throat. I blew my load within five minutes one of those times. It seemed to surprise her. It probably pleased her that the sex was over for a day and then she had a day off, so about forty-eight hours until she would once again feel my burning infected semen inside of her.

I had to carefully think of how I was going to go about it while jerking off in a bubble bath one evening. Rose scent filled my nostrils and relaxed me. My mind wasn't on her trachea ring, it was on her fat rolls and titty-fucking her. But thinking of it followed by some mind-wandering helped me come up with my plan.

I needed to drug her. She was, and still is, much bigger than me. I was not confident in my ability to keep her pinned down while I fucked her life away even with my body exceptionally toned due to hours spent at the gym bemoaning my next to non-existent sex life. Drugs offered the solution.

I knew I couldn't get her to swallow a handful of pills. And she'd be able to tell if I chopped sleeping tablets into a fine powder and poured them into her tea, arguing that the funny taste is a new type of sweetener because I was worried about her weight. She'd never fall for something like that. Although, she never noticed the taste of laxatives I would sometimes spike her drinks with. But it wasn't worth the risk. And I would need to keep her drugged for a few days at the very least because I wanted all of my jerk-off fantasies to come true.

Ten

It was she who gave me the idea for how to drug her through. She was sat in her festering old armchair that once belonged to her late first husband (who probably died of boredom) and still had the stale smell of years of his farts watching Nat Geo. A documentary about drugs was next in the listing. Something she wouldn't normally watch but she had dozed off. I watched intently though while she drooled down herself. On that night I absorbed information on opiates like a great giant sponge plunged into a bucket of warm soapy water. If I injected her with heroin in her sleep she wouldn't be able to bat the needle away.

She might wake up. I need to get the dosage just right. Too much will kill her; too little and she'll only feel the needle going into her vein with no effect on her then she might phone the police and tell them. She was too prude to take street drugs but she did take prescribed painkillers. And she was overweight. Dosage was a tricky thing. I spent many hours sat on the toilet with shit drying to my arse on my smart phone trying to figure out how much to give her.

Then I had to find a needle and a drug dealer. Needles were easy to get from the internet but I didn't want to get mail-order drugs. That could alert the police to me. I don't take drugs and I never have done. I didn't think I knew anybody who did but a few poised questions and I discovered a friend who I thought I knew well was partial to a spot of cocaine at the weekends. He was able to hook me up with heroin and didn't ask too many questions.

When I finally plucked up the courage to inject her it was terrible. I sat in a cold sweat on the bed next to her propped up on pillows. I pretended to sleep. She always fell asleep after me so I had to wait and pretend to snore propped up on my feather pillows until she stopped tossing and turning. She finally settled on a position that pulled me closer to her due to her immense weight.

My hands were shaking. My entire body was shaking as it sunk closer to her. I'm rather surprised and rather grateful that it didn't wake her up. She must have been really tired that night.

I managed to reach into my bedside table without waking her. She never looked in it. I had the drug dealer prepare the heroin for me. I didn't want to be messing around in the dark knowing I would be anxious and shaking and sweating. This was my dream and it was coming true, I wasn't going to let inefficient knowledge of drugs ruin it.

I wasn't sure I'd be able to hit her vein but I did. She woke up when the needle went in but she soon drifted to a state between consciousness and dreamland. I found the ease in which she went out rather unnerving. Something would go wrong, somehow, somewhere in the course of this. Nothing was that easy.

Eleven

Next I had to get her in the basement. She was, and still is, a very big lady. Beautiful but huge. Without any sleep I had to come up with a plan then and there. I should have thought it through during a mindless day at the office.

I decided to drag her in the sheet. If the sheet decided it didn't want to tear apart, stretched by her weight. I know drugging her with such ease was too simple and that something somewhere would go wrong.

I threw the duvet and pillows onto the floor and lifted the fitted edges off the bed. My lovely wife stared blankly at the ceiling. I'm not sure if she felt anything resembling anxiety deep down inside. She might have. But I don't think she was aware of what was going on.

I didn't want the thin sheet to tear or for her to fall out of it when I was dragging. I tied the edges around her midsection just beneath her braless breasts. They sagged over the knot.

Drool escaped her open lips and ran down her face. It didn't smell very pleasant. It entered my nose and embraced my sinuses without leaning close. I wanted to lick it off her. So I did. The taste was exactly like the smell. Wet and sour with hints of stickiness. She didn't flinch when I went in for a second taste.

Without her voice box she was speechless. I liked her that way. She never had anything interesting to say. I pulled the sheet up the back of her head so her lovely grey locks wouldn't be pulled out – they were my second favourite part of her, after her trachea ring. The elastic pulled across her forehead. I hoped it would stay.

Moving from the bedroom downstairs to the basement was much easier than I envisioned. It was another thing that I wished I had thought through while set to some mind-numbing task in the office. But it worked out.

I actually managed to cradle and lift my sheet-wrapped obese wife off the bed. I think it was more to do with a sudden rush of adrenaline rather than excessive hours working out due to my lack of a sex life (until recently).

I put her on the floor to save my strength for the stairs. The thick carpet, so soft on my callused feet, made things a little more difficult in terms of dragging her.

I knew I should have put my foot down about laminate flooring but she really wanted to keep the carpet because her late husband had put it in. I caved. I shouldn't have but I did. She was so happy that I let her keep her precious carpet that I pissed on it on a regular basis like a ritual. I wanted to get a cat as well because nothing smells worse than a male cat's urine but I couldn't find an adult one with his balls intact. The entire house, except the kitchen and bathrooms were covered in the same bronzed green carpet.

I'll rip it out when I'm done with her. Smooth floors would have meant I made it to the basement without becoming tired. As it was her obese-form glided across the carpet with an ease that surprised me but still required far too much use of my muscles.

I didn't want her head to spilt open going down the stairs. She could die from a head injury or snapped neck entirely by accident and ruin my dreams. That would be just like her.

I wasn't sure I wanted to fall while carrying her either as it was entirely possible that I would lose my footing. But I feel I would drop her first and it would increase my chances of landing on top of her and having some cushioning. The worst that would happen if I fell backwards would be bruising my arse. But I could live with that.

I decided to carry her. I wish I encouraged her to keep up with her Weight Watchers meetings. It would have made the task a bit easier. I liked to imagine myself fucking her stomach rolls though. They were so soft and squeezy. My cock would fit in oh-so nicely between them.

Something she would never allow me to do. I should have forced myself on the moody bitch but she would have phoned the police and that would have ruined my bigger plans. I didn't want that. So I would use the stomach fat in my jerk off fantasies. Weight Watchers ran the risk of destroying that. I didn't want to jerk off while thinking of her trachea ring too often – the fantasy could ruin the reality when the time arrived by building my expectations too high.

So I carried her obese semi-conscious body down the stairs. Her fat feet rubbed against the wall. It made progress slow. My arms creaked beneath her weight. At least fat weighs less than muscle; I have that to be grateful for. But, the fat spilled over my arms and her arse-fat dragged so low it hit my knees on the way down.

I nearly lost my temper and threw her the rest of the way but I didn't want to break her neck. I wanted to fuck her dying breath out of her trachea ring. I couldn't do that if she died of a neck injury at the bottom of the stairs.

I didn't care if one or both of her ankles snapped. In fact, it would make keeping her in the basement easier. But neither did. The fat must have protected them. My arms and back were sore when I reached the bottom.

I dropped her on the carpeted floor. Her eyes flew open and then fell into the dazed glazed look of someone who is high. I wanted to kick her but I was afraid my foot would become caught in her fat and I would have to cut it off to save myself. People might ask questions then.

I dragged her through the ground floor to the kitchen. The colour of the carpet was sickening. I didn't like looking at it but I was becoming too tired to look anywhere else. It was like I was lugging all my work-out equipment behind me in a big smelly bundle.

Twelve

Beneath the kitchen table was the trap door leading to the basement. Her late husband wouldn't allow it to be boarded up – he used it to store root vegetables like the Americans with unfinished root cellars. I don't know how he managed to keep the humidity down enough to do this but I guess he did from what my lovely has told me and I found a potato with many eyes down there so I didn't doubt her story.

My lovely wife's sheet wrapped fat rolled with smoothness and ease across the kitchen. Her late husband had put down smooth new tiles before he died. I wish it rolled with this much ease across the rest of the ground floor. It would have if I had only put my foot down about the carpets. Or if her late husband didn't have such appalling taste.

I dumped her near the table and pushed it away from the trap door, knocking down a chair in the process. I didn't think the neighbours were awake to hear but it resulted in some muscle tenseness for a few seconds to make sure. I didn't hear them so I assumed they were still tucked up snoring in their beds, farting in their sleep. Tipping over a chair was hardly a crime but these were nosey bastards who read far too much into everything.

I opened the door. I didn't trust the stairs. My lovely wife was so very heavy. I wasn't even sure the stairs could take my weight, let alone both of us going down together. Old wooden things, I'm surprised her first husband never replaced them with something more sturdy.

Humid air, the same humid air that warped the stairs, crept up the hole and gave me a hug before moving and defusing through the rest of the kitchen. It smelt of decay and was like a pleasant perfume to my nose. I wanted to inhale it forever but I had a task to finish before my lovely wife regained consciousness.

Buzzing flies from the maggots I planted down there a month ago in putrid meat flew out into the fresh air of the kitchen. I would need to put up fly paper through-out the house before the neighbours noticed. Enough stayed in the basement to lay their eggs in her trachea ring. That was enough for me.

Thirteen

I decided the best course of action would be for me to drag her down on the greasy mattress I found at the roadside two months ago infested with bed-bugs and fleas. As my attempt to get a cat failed and we had no other pets the fleas were probably all dead. I left her heaped fat form on the kitchen floor while I went to retrieve it.

Her late first husband had some sense because he had a light installed in the basement. I pulled the string and the bare high power bulb clicked into life above me. The flies didn't seem to like it but I didn't care.

The mattress seemed to have grown some mould since I dumped it down there one day when she was having tea and cakes with her equally fat girlfriends. She never went into the basement and didn't realise that I did. I wasn't worried about her finding it. I could have hidden anything down there without her finding out.

It had come off a single bed. I wished it was foam for the moving but then I thought her flab deserved to be poked by rusty springs. A little more effort will be worth it in the long run. I wanted to hear the springs creak as I fuck her trachea ring. I wanted to see spring-shaped red spots and maybe even blood in her flesh.

I dragged it up the stairs that didn't seem solid enough. They were wide planks of wood with only about a twelve inch step between them. If I trusted them it would have been easy to carry her down. Even easier than carrying her down the stairs in the house because there was only a wall on one side and only a thin bannister for her fat feet to hit.

I dragged the mattress up hoping none of the springs would get caught on the possible rotten wood. Even a single mattress is a bulky item but it fit while lying flat as I knew it would. I plopped it down on the kitchen floor next to my lovely wife.

Gas must have been seeping out of her anus while I was down there as she was engulfed in a toxic cloud upon my return. Of all the times for her arse to leak, why did it have to be right when I wanted to bring her into the basement? She could have the courtesy to have waited until I had her chained up down there.

Flies had already landed on her. They weren't impacted by the smell in the same way. I'm rather sure that they enjoy wallowing in terrible odours that have the potential to kill a human, disgusting little creatures that they are.

I picked up the chair I had knocked over and moved it as far away from my lovely wife as the kitchen would allow. I would have to wait for the gas to defuse in the atmosphere otherwise I would risk passing out getting her down the stairs. She may regain consciousness and phone the police leaving me chained up in her place. I opened the kitchen window for good measure.

Some of the flies flew out but the basement was still teeming with them. As long as there were enough to lay their eggs in her trachea ring it didn't matter.

Fourteen

Maggots have always turned me on. I don't know what it is about them that makes me hard but they are fucking amazing. Ensuring enough time for flies to lay eggs would guarantee me an erection.

I have never been able to convince a woman to let me push them into her vagina before I fuck her (or after, for that matter). Not even a hooker I offered to pay double. The hooker seemed offended and stormed out of the alley where I intended to fuck her with her pants around her ankles and her skirt hitched up.

I filled a fuck-cup with them once but fuck-cups are always expensive and purchasing one made me feel like such a loser, I didn't repeat the experience even though it was the best sex I had ever had. When I inserted my dick a maggot found its way up my urethra. Nothing had ever felt so good.

Fuck cups can only be reused if one uses a condom, obviously I had no intention of using a condom when the fuck cup was filled with precious maggots.

I once tried to convince a dominatrix to give me an enema with maggots that had been liquefied in a blender. She refused and stormed out of the hotel room after untying me. She was so disgusted she forgot to collect my payment. I'm glad she untied me. That would have been awkward when the maid came in.

I knew I could never ask my prudish wife to do such a thing. She would have never agreed and thrown me out into the street completely naked, there-by destroying my chances of fucking her trachea ring. I might have been able to charm my way back in but it was a risk I wasn't willing to take.

Fifteen

I watched as more flies landed on her. She flinched silently when one landed on her dazed and glazed eye. She blinked a little. It made me wonder if it was nearly time for her next dosage of heroin.

I approached her being sure to breathe through my mouth. I didn't want to risk passing out. If I passed out too close to her the toxic fumes from her arse could kill me. I don't want to die.

She didn't bat the needle away. As I said already, my main desire is to fuck her trachea ring. The last thing I wanted was for her to die of a heroin overdose before I had the chance.

The air in the kitchen was stirred by a breeze coming in through the window. It was safe to breathe properly, just about. I didn't want to take any risks though. Her arse fumes were well known to be toxic.

I went back to my chair and watched the flies land on her for another ten minutes. None flew out the open window. I guess my lovely wife offered better pickings than outside. I didn't agree with them, I've experienced the compost.

Sixteen

My lovely wife had gone to Butlins with her friends for a girls' weekend. I was left alone. Jerking off while fantasising about fucking her fat rolls and then eating dick cheese failed to keep me entertained. All the hookers in the area had been warned about me and no one would see me, especially as I didn't have those genital warts treated by that point.

The sun was blazing down on the garden. I had all the windows in the house open and was sat in my piss stained y-fronts at the kitchen table picking ear wax out and wiping it on apples in the fruit bowl. I looked out the open kitchen window and there it was, covered in flies and wasps, the compost heap demanding my love. The wind was blowing in the right direction, my nostrils and the house was filled with the scent of ripe summer decay.

The first twitches of an erection threatened to tear through my piss stained y-fronts. I stood up and looked out the open door. The neighbours were at work and even if they weren't I didn't care.

I walked across the yellowed grass. Each blade stabbed my bare feet but it couldn't break the rough skin. And even if it could, I was about to receive wasp stings to my cock, pain didn't bother me.

As I walked I pulled down my pants and left them on the grass. I was in a trance. I wanted to run and dive into the compost but I was held back to savour the moment. I could almost separate each and every individual thing that was thrown in there over the course of the winter and spring. My cock wanted to burst at the scent of mouldy orange peels.

Thunder sounded in the distance and the wind kicked up the exact second I reached my destination. I bent over and picked up two handfuls of the stuff. Festering old lettuce, or what I thought was lettuce, became stuck in my nail. I sucked it off.

My cock felt like it was going to explode. I needed to pound that compost. But I wanted to savour every moment of it.

Thunder boomed. A storm was approaching. The air went still (as it does just before a bad summer storm). Complete silence spread through the fields and approached the houses facing away from them. It spread through my compost heap and even the flies and wasps stopped buzzing for a second or two.

With each approaching boom, my cock tingled with anticipation. This moment would be the height of my sex life until I could find someone to cater to my needs. I wanted it to last forever but knew it would pass in the same way as the storm.

I walked up to the compost heap and plunged my dick straight in. It met with a wasp which nearly brought on ejaculation right there and then but I held it in. My scrotum was stung. I wanted the wasps to sting right through it but none did.

I pushed in and out of that compost, meeting with either the same wasp or many different wasps. Flies landed on me and my arse was stung. Only compost found its way up my dildo loosened arsehole, which was rather disappointing.

The storm rolled in closer. I didn't want to cum until I felt hail on my back. My cock, however, had different ideas. It was a battle of wills. My brain who wanted heightened pleasure versus my cock who wanted instant gratification.

I slowed down and thought of my lovely wife's eight children but that threatened to take away my erection entirely. And maybe even make my balls crawl up inside of me. Then I was stung again and again and my hard-on returned.

Thunder boomed. I could hear the rain and hail pelting the earth before I felt it on me. Then my back was hit with millions of tiny stings all at once. These weren't from the wasps but the hail I was waiting for. It was a magical moment of ejaculation as I climaxed, pulled out and ran for cover. A wasp followed me and stung me on the back of the neck.

I arrived inside stinking of compost and cum. I wanted to savour it but knew my lovely wife would complain when she arrived home if the smell wasn't gone and I detest cleaning so I ran upstairs for the shower rather than jumping into bed and jerking off while reliving the memory.

Seventeen

My cock tingled looking down at my lovely wife from my safe spot, thinking of the compost. I thought it would be safe to move her semi-conscious body to the mattress so I would be one step closer to turning some more fantasies into reality.

I went over to her. Her arse was still leaking toxins into the atmosphere but with the window open and a breeze coming in it seemed okay to move her. I was able to put her on the mattress ready to go downstairs. She seemed heavier then. Maybe because I was close to the last part of the task. I dragged her flabby form from under the arms onto the festering mattress. Flies danced around us.

I wanted to move her before the drug wore off but I didn't know if that was going to happen or when. Her arse could be considered an environmental hazard. Once I start going down those stairs the air will become still and ventilation in the basement near enough non-existent. Her toxic gas could suffocate me before I have a chance to fuck her trachea ring.

I must invest in a gas mask if I don't want the neighbours to find our decaying bodies when the flies become too heavy and threaten to over-take their house and garden. I can imagine the headlines. Man found covered in flies with penis in wife's trachea ring. I don't want to be remembered that way. It was too late to turn back and wait for a day in which I have a gas mask. I didn't fancy carrying her back upstairs and to bed and there was no way I would be able to convince her that it was all just some terrible dream.

I should have encouraged her to have a shit before bed. Then she wouldn't have an invisible cloud of gas surrounding her. Or at least, she wouldn't smell as bad. But it was too late for should haves.

Sometimes I would force her to eat papaya so she would shit before bed and I could sleep with the window shut. Otherwise I wouldn't wake up the next morning. That's probably how her first husband died but I never enquired.

More flies landed on my lovely wife. Perhaps they were already laying their eggs in her. I knew I would disturb them when I went to move her into the basement. I wish I wouldn't but there were much more waiting for her down there.

She didn't smell as bad when I went in close. She had stopped farting long enough to bring her into the basement, which would require me being close to her (although hopefully not her arse).

I faced two choices: I could push the mattress down the stairs or I could pull it. Pushing meant that my lovely wife couldn't fall on top of me and suffocate me. Pulling it meant that she would be more unlikely to fall because I would be more likely to catch her. Pulling it would mean I would be further away from her arse and its toxic gas releases.

Unmarried woman with trachea rings are a rarity – I wanted to get this right the first time. No, I needed to get this right the first time; another unmarried woman with a trachea ring wasn't very likely to come my way again.

The back of my mind, where I hide my inner child, used this moment to speak up; sit on the mattress with her and use upper body strength to get to the basement like a toboggan. I usually tuned out my inner child, nothing good ever came from it, but this time I thought it was onto something.

Flies landed on her while I pondered. I needed to do something before her arse started up again or she shit herself. Or, even worse, she woke up.

Sitting with her on the mattress might be the best idea. I could ensure she safely reached the bottom without getting crushed. And I could avoid her arse-fumes.

I lined the mattress up with the trap door. My lovely wife stared at the ceiling, oblivious to my efforts. Flies buzzed around looking for fresh meat.

The hardest part would be pulling it over the edge and through the hole. I peeked into the gloom. Tingles of anxiety hugged my chest, taunting me and reminding me that this is the most difficult part of the task.

Our weight will be dispersed on the mattress so I wouldn't have to worry about the stairs collapsing. That is the only non-anxiety-inducing thing to come from this part. So much to worry about; so much that can go wrong. I need to focus (on her trachea ring).

I sat on the edge of the mattress. That didn't seem to work. I laid down flat on my stomach, my feet resting on my lovely wife's fat folds and pulled on the top stair. That resulted in movement. I would have to be careful not to hurt my arms.

I reached the second stair with my finger tip and went another foot into the humid gloom. My biggest fear was a spring becoming caught or a lethal release from her rear end. Neither happened.

When the mattress reached the last stair I stood onto the concrete floor and pulled it the rest of the way. It hurt my back to bend over but I was nearly there. Nearly at the chains where I could secure her incase she woke up while I was at work.

Eighteen

My lovely wife stared straight up at the ceiling, her mouth open and her tongue poking out. A fly landed on it. She twitched but didn't bring it back into her mouth. I wished she would. But then, I would also wish for a camera to take a picture I would never be able to show anyone outside of the deepest, darkest, invitation-only internet forums.

Once flat on the basement floor the mattress was easy to move. The humidity and dampness seemed to lubricate it. It still hurt to bend over but at least it moved with ease. And I still wasn't banned from the massage and fuck massage parlours.

Flies buzzed, their resting spots disturbed. I pushed the mattress into a far corner. Someone had installed metal brackets into the walls. I wanted to chain her incase she became fully conscious while I was at work and escaped and notified the police.

I pushed and pulled the mattress laden down with the weight of my obese wife until it was an inch away from the brackets. I wish I could use Japanese rope bondage instead of chains but if that were the case I wouldn't be chaining my lovely wife up in the basement.

Nineteen

With her secured to the wall I didn't want to leave her by herself just yet. I wasn't ready to fuck her trachea ring but my main jerk off fantasy was about to come true.

Flies buzzed all around me. None landed on me. My sex-starved cock was already erect. I pulled off my pyjama bottoms and discarded them on the floor, where they'd stay.

I managed to convince my lovely wife that sleeping topless really is a comfort issue. It took months but the night I brought her down here I was without a shirt so I didn't have one to take off and discard on the floor.

Not like she would have noticed anything. Her blank eyes stared at the rotted wooden beams that served as a ceiling. They were covered with flies.

I disturbed a big juicy spider when I rolled her on her side. With this amount of flies, spiders could easily become as obese as my lovely wife. I was a bit peckish so I tried to pick it up and eat it but it scurried away too fast.

I lifted her white vest, stained yellow around the armpits that served as her night shirt. She really needed a new one, or one in a darker colour but that didn't matter anymore. There was no point in removing her pyjama bottoms. It wasn't her tight vagina that I was after.

On her side stretched out her stomach rolls didn't look fuckable so I moved her legs bringing them under her until she was in foetal position. That left me with a selection of places to plant my dick.

My balls bulged and pulsed. It was amazing that I didn't blow my load while I examined her stomach rolls by prodding them with my fingers. She didn't move while I poked and even fisted one area. I wanted the best place for my jerk-off fantasy to come true.

I choose my spot just beneath her braless breasts. It was nice and sweaty beneath them. Fungus probably grew there. My cock would like it.

I sat on top of her like I was mounting a pony. Then I leant forward. Her blubber shifted to fit the weight and muscle tone of my perfectly sculpted body. Springs creaked underneath. My cock found entrance where her fat connected.

I pushed in and out finally gaining sexual release. I tried to hold in my orgasm but it was pointless. There was no way I would have due to being denied pleasurable sex for so long. I thought my cock would explode. The river of jiz seemed like it never wanted to stop. When it finally did I pulled away.

I felt sleepy and wanted an hour or so kip before I had to get ready for work. I didn't bother to wipe away my semen or pull down her shirt. Flies landed on it. That was the last thing I saw as I went up the stairs.

I left the light on incase she woke up. I didn't want her becoming confused. She should have the mental capacity to recognise her own basement. She's lived in the house for thirty-odd years.

Twenty

The worms are a nice touch. I picked them up from the angling shop I have to walk past on my way to work. I'm glad I bought them. I wish I bought two containers. I like to watch them squirm out of her trachea ring when I can see through the flies.

I sat on the stairs, not even worried about them collapsing, on that first day after work watching as she struggled to regain some sort of consciousness. No matter how much she tried it was never successful. My lovely wife was a submissive woman and if she wasn't I would have emotionally beat any dominance out of her long before I proposed. Submissive woman can't find the strength to fight.

Maybe when I poured the worms with the few inches of cool moist soil between her fat rolls she was able to feel them squirm and it tickled and started to wake her. Maybe the drug was wearing off. Maybe she was already building up a resistance. Maybe it was a combination of everything and the submissive nature of my lovely wife was about to repressed by something awful (although sure to have much amusement).

My seat on the too soft stairs didn't provide prime worm viewing conditions or even prime wife viewing conditions as she was shaded in the gloom and I wanted to see every expression etched onto her aging face. I wish it did. Then I wouldn't need to get up for a closer look at my lovely wife and risk an inhalation of arse-fumes.

The stairs didn't creak when I stood up – only dry wood seems to do that but I felt them groan somewhere deep inside the moistness and it made me wonder how many more trips into the basement I would be allowed to make. Once done with my lovely wife and her beautiful trachea ring I planned on the basement becoming her final resting place by sealing up the trap door. But I didn't want the stairs to collapse before then.

I needed to put up fly paper before I could watch the internal argument in my lovely wife manifest externally on her face. I don't want flies to lead to my discovery. The neighbours could phone environmental health and report them. Then I'll have some sort of health inspector around here and he (or she in this day and age) might want to look in the basement. I wish I could leave them for another day to ensure enough eggs end up in my lovely wife but I don't want to take the chance.

I hung fly paper from the beams serving as a ceiling. Her late and great first husband didn't think to install a ceiling down here in his special place. I bet he had the concrete poured in to hide all the bodies he buried beneath the dirt floor though. It wouldn't surprise me. Living with her for all those years would drive anyone to murder and possibly forgetfulness leading to a lack of a ceiling.

I'll have to be careful to duck walking beneath them so they don't get caught in my hair. I don't want to have to shave it off. That would be a major inconvenience and my idiotic work colleagues would want to rub my head for good luck. My lovely wife should have had the foresight to move into a converted farm house with the nearest neighbours half a mile away. Then I wouldn't have to bother with fly paper and remembering to duck.

I went over to her. Her eyes had lost their distant dazed and glazed look. They followed me but she didn't put in any effort to move. I wondered if she had even tried to while I was at work. I doubt it; only her laziness tops her submissiveness.

I had to breathe through my mouth. If too much of the odour went up my nose I would vomit. I didn't like smelling it but I really enjoyed tasting it. If I didn't enjoy the succulent flavour so much I would snort her sweat and shit and vomit all over my lovely wife.

I had her next heroin dose ready but if possible I wanted to fuck her without giving it to her. I wanted her to feel my cock pulse against her. I wanted her to be disgusted by it and my sick fetishes that I act out on her. I wanted her to be shocked and horrified at the same time. I wanted her to really know the man she had married. She was my lovely wife, she should satisfy me; whenever, wherever and however I want.

Twenty-one

I stroked her greying locks off her face. She seemed tense but I suppose anyone waking up to discover that they are covered in dry flaking semen and being eaten by worms while flies planted their eggs on a mouldy mattress in their own basement would be. If she was too tense I might break one of her bones which would cause her agony in her remaining days. That sounded like a good idea but not just yet; I wanted to keep her whole as long as possible.

I ran my finger behind her ear in search of the place that makes her relax. I found it. I rubbed it gently. It didn't have the impact I had hoped. I could almost hear her bones cracking open beneath the pressure she was putting them under.

Perhaps a foot massage. She had never allowed me to give her one before. Every time I tried she kicked my hands away; sometimes scratching me with her yellowed toenails that curled upwards, always tearing her socks and never becoming ingrown.

I moved my hands down her wobbly body disturbing flies as I did so. They didn't seem all that bothered. My hands were nearly caught in her fat rolls. I wouldn't be surprised, if I allowed her to live, if they grew teeth and start consuming anything put in between them.

I was tempted to pull down her pyjama bottoms and stick my unlubricated middle finger in her anus but I resisted. She would have really fought her submissive nature and try to fart on me if I did that. That would result in a beating.

It was like my hand was smoothing the creases in her pyjama bottoms as it moved towards her feet. They were soiled. She must have shit herself when I was at work. Her faeces didn't smell as bad as that toxic gas she would release. I never could work that out. Her shit would act as some sort of lubricant, I'm sure.

My hands arrived at her feet. Hard skin covered her heels. Flies wouldn't land on that part. There would be no point. It would be like landing on dry concrete. Not even the humidity in the basement which made it seem like an extension of a tropical rainforest softened her heels.

I rubbed my thumb along the callused skin. It was doubtful she could feel it. I should have brought something down to shave it off and reveal soft young skin close to nerve endings underneath but my foresight in these matters wasn't so good. It never has been which is rather unfortunate.

I moved my thumb along the arch. She kicked but it wasn't as aggressive as a younger, less-weighty, less submissive prisoner would have given. The kick was a disappointment, actually.

This part of her foot isn't as callused so it must be more sensitive, even through the layer of fat that add a few shoe sizes to her feet. I pinched at it. I know obese people hate having their blubber pinched and prodded. She kicked again. It, once again, failed to impress me.

I grabbed her foot. She was going to have this foot massage before I injected her with more heroin whether she tried to resist or not. She needed to feel it and embrace it. She tried to struggle away but was too weak.

She doesn't really have ankles to speak of. I don't think she ever has. She was too heavy. Pictures of her in childhood revealed a little whale in a lacy dress. I'm surprised she was able to squeeze herself into a princess gown with matching corset for her first wedding. Back fat in the pictures looked like extra boobs incase her late and great first husband wanted to hold onto those if he ever fucked her from behind (which seems rather unlikely). I had to press hard to find her ankle bone. She didn't seem to like that so I pressed harder – all the inner rage of never being allowed to give her a foot massage bubbled to the surface. I bit down on the inside of my cheek drawing the coppery taste of blood. If she didn't have that cushioning of blubber I think I may have broken her ankle.

I ran my thumb over her arch next. She really didn't seem to like that so I gripped her foot tighter and pressed my thumb harder. I pinched her ankle fat with my other hand.

A foot massage can be a very sensual thing. Beads of sweat accumulated on my skin as I rubbed and fought off my lovely wife's kicking. An erection grew in my trousers. I don't know if it was the foot rub or her resisting that turned me on. Maybe it was a bit of both. I planned on sorting it out right after her massage.

A fly landed on my hand as I rubbed. I didn't mind. In a basement filled with flies wanting to lay their precious eggs it was like a friend saying 'I'm doing what you've asked of me'. It soon flew away but it was a nice gesture of love and warmth, something my lovely wife would never do.

I wanted to suck the dirt and lint from underneath her toes but I knew I had to wait until the time was right. She might need to be drugged first but I rather she wasn't. That way I can be confident she'll be able to feel my smooth slobbering tongue. She must have known what I had planned for she started a fresh batch of kicking. I'm surprised that she found the strength. She had been down there for nearly twenty hours without any food to feed her fat arse at that point. She must have been living off her fat reserves; goodness knows there were enough of them.

I rubbed the joints on her toes and pulled each individual one towards me with a slowness that reminded me of a snail. She actually seemed to like that. Her feet must get so sore carrying around her weight and she never before allowed me the opportunity to give her a sensual foot massage until she had been off them for nearly twenty hours. I felt like I was pulling out years of soreness though. She calmed down a bit.

Until, as expected, she didn't like it when I wrapped my mouth around her big toe and began sucking. She kicked but I grabbed her ankles and rolled my tongue between her big toe and its neighbour. It was a tight squeeze – like fitting my cock into her vagina. I kept it there. Her feeble kicks provided the thrusting movement.

My cock grew harder but I wanted to suck each of her fat toes before fucking her. I moved my mouth to the next and sucked off the sour salt.

Flies landed in the pool of saliva beneath her feet on the festering mattress. I wanted them to land on her. My saliva mixed with essence of feet was a temptation too strong for them to resist.

Her yellowed uneven toenail scraped against my tongue and the roof of my mouth. I could nearly feel bacteria entering the cut that would later lead to a minor infection killed by excessive use of mouth wash. I don't know what was on her feet but my tongue went a slight tint of green and grew a little layer of fur. If I knew then about the minor infection I would have slapped her and told her that she should take better care of herself.

If she would hold still then I could have rubbed her feet while I sucked. I don't think I tickled her; I think she found the sensation uncomfortable more than anything else. She worked herself into a sweat, which wasn't difficult given the humidity. It would serve as my lubricant when I fucked her, wherever on her body I decided to stick my dick in.

Droplets of urine reached my nose. It smelt fresh yet very strong. It did nothing to cover up the stale piss. And soon the fresh piss would join the odours of the stale. I made a mental note to bring her something to drink. I wanted her stay alive until the time came for me to fuck away her dying breath. I considered hooking her up to a catheter and connecting it to her mouth but I wasn't sure if that would kill her and didn't want to take the risk – woman with trachea rings were such a rarity.

Her toes were leaving me with a taste so sour my tongue felt like it was trying to implode. I decided to stop for the day. I planned on washing them first the following day.

Twenty-two

I stood up and looked down on her. If it wasn't for that lovely trachea ring she would disgust me to the point that I would vomit on her. The trachea ring was her only enduring feature and the only reason I tolerated her bullshit for so long.

She had fright etched across her face. It made me wish that I carried a pocket knife. Then I could cut those lines in permanently and have her mummified after her death so there would be a reminder that would last forever, much like a diamond but even better and much more fun.

She was shaking. I'm not sure if that was due to fear or drug withdrawal. I'm not sure if she was aware she was doing it. I didn't care. I liked paying witness to her distress. It turned me on to the point that I thought my balls might explode and splatter creamy white everywhere.

Instead of fucking the folds of her flesh I thought I might make it rain jiz on her and the flies. She never let me do it before. It would be nice to carry out the act before she died.

Then I could dump the contents of the worm container on my lovely wife and between her rolls of fat; moist dark dirt as well as big fat juicy pink night crawlers. I put down my container of worms on the concrete out of her range of sight – I wanted them to be a surprise. I didn't want her to know what the cold slimy things wriggling on her were. I wanted my lovely wife to assume the worst.

I pulled down my trousers and pants. They dropped to my ankles and landed on the dirty concrete, exposing my legs to the full-force of the humidity for the first time – the water droplets were instantaneous.

My cock bounced upwards at its joy of being released. I grabbed it and squeezed. Pre-ejaculation oozed out and acted as a lubricant for my hand going back and forth. In future trips I may want to bring some lotion down to the basement with me. None of the pre-cum dripped onto my lovely wife.

I was saving my load of creamy white for her. I knew it wouldn't take long and predicted one of those orgasms that left one crippled for up to half an hour afterwards. I've only ever had those by jerking-off; woman just weren't good enough for me, even professional whores.

For someone who didn't express any interest in sex or know anything about it, she seemed to know what was going to happen. She tried to squirm out of range. She has probably never had cum dripped onto her flesh (except when I used her fat rolls as a masturbator last night but that doesn't count because she wasn't conscious). She probably never even realised it is white in colour or that sperm aren't visible to the naked eye.

In all her sober struggles she never managed to pull down her pyjama top – already turning more yellow with the first signs of decay. Her breasts sagged and bounced. I could only tell they were separate to the fat rolls due to their dark brown nipples that fed eight babies.

I stood over her. I wanted my jiz to land on bare skin. I wanted her to feel it and embrace the warmth and stickiness. I could feel it building, but I suppose it had been building for a long time, or since the night before.

But this was the orgasm to over-shadow all other orgasms. Since I discovered I had a penis and it was for more than pissing I had been denied decent orgasmic sex. For a while I even tried men thinking I might possibly be gay but they weren't any better than woman or animals. My hand was my best friend and this was the best way to jerk-off.

I had finally sucked on her toes. A lot of women enjoy their toes being sucked and slobbered on, but not my lovely wife. The sour taste didn't disappear from my mouth until I brushed my teeth later on in the evening before I retired to bed. That taste heightened my pleasure.

Her eyes dilated. She tried to squirm away from the firing range. It only served to make me cum before I wanted to but the release was immediate. She should have been slapped for that one as it was entirely her fault that I blew my load early.

I thought the waterfall of creamy white would never let up. It rained upon her. She tried to squirm away clicking the chains but no matter where she moved semen landed on her. It was like an uncontrollable hose. I couldn't direct where it would land. Some splattered on her forehead where it would later dry and flake off.

Flies buzzed and landed in it while it was still squirting out of me. There were so many flies and so much jiz that flies drowned in it. I left them there to die on my lovely wife. I would later eat their little dirty bodies – my cum acted as salt.

I collapsed to my knees on the festering mattress next to her. My cock was still in my hand and jiz still oozed out, covering me too in sticky creamy white. I licked my fingers. I loved the taste of my own semen.

My lovely wife squirmed to the other side of the mattress. Springs creaked and her chains rattled in a beautiful melody of her predicament. She wouldn't dare put up a fight even though I was vulnerable then, she was too submissive and lacked any sort of fight or flight response. It was a bit of a turn off. I wanted to see her squirm; it could have quickened my recovery.

I wished I collapsed near her head so I could have run my fingers through her stringy greasy hair while my strength returned. A little bit of hair stroking would have relaxed her a bit. My lovely wife couldn't resist it. It was the only place she liked to be touched, apart from behind her ear.

Twenty-three

I fell forward, my head landed in her shit covered arse. I could smell it, even though it had quite clearly dried, through her pastel pyjama bottoms. Her pyjamas weren't stained a shade of brown which told me it was dry when it left her arse.

I inhaled deeply. The smell was intoxicatingly perfect. If I hadn't spent myself a few seconds previous I would have grown an instant erection.

My lovely wife would have one believe she shat roses, even though there was no denying the toxic clouds that would leak out of her arse on a regular basis. Women, or more precisely women like my lovely wife, don't shit. Ever. If I was at home she would never use the toilet. She went entire weekends without empting her bowels (unless I spiked something with laxatives, which I sometimes did; sometimes to relieve the smell of her farts, sometimes for my own personal amusement).

I exhaled invisible particles of her dried shit as a plan began to form. She hadn't eaten anything in hours. She must be hungry. So hungry she would eat anything and everything. She needs to stuff her face to keep her lovely flabby curves.

I didn't want her to be as high as a kite and some other place while she ate her own shit and recovered those calories lost when it escaped out of her arse. I wanted her to know what she was doing and where the shit had come from. I wanted her to admit that she shit and it stank.

I would need to make a full recovery. My lovely wife, as submissive as she was, would put up a fight on this one. It wouldn't be a big fight. But a fight, none-the-less. I needed all my strength to take her on.

I laid there as I waited for strength to return. The flies buzzed around. I absently licked jiz off my fingers (it was still warm).

I focused on inhaling the scent of her shit and the taste of my creamy white. I wanted to taste her shit but I didn't want her to acknowledge she did it (yet).

The shit combined with other smells to quell my growing impatience. I would fail if I attempted before making a complete recovery. I didn't want to fail. I had to be patient. Patience was a virtue I was known to possess.

I waited years before I brought my lovely wife down here and chained her up. I waited months before proposing even though we both knew we would get married. Patience would lead to my date with her trachea ring.

I don't think my lovely wife realised she had shit her pants. Her denial of body functions was such that even her subconscious would pretend it didn't happen. She might pay some sort of vague attention to it when she was in the act but that's about it.

I always wanted to watch her shit. Maybe later I'll bring her something more sustaining to eat so I can sit down here and watch as it passes through her and out her arsehole. I made a mental note but I soon forgot and she never did get something that hadn't already passed through her to eat before she died. Her last meal was that turd I fed to her.

Each inhale brought a different combination of smells to my nose. One breath and the odour of her strong urine was heavier than the scent of her dried shit. I exhaled and it went away. Maybe she had pissed herself again. In the next inhale I caught a whiff of her sweat and my jiz. Then next one brought dried shit-flakes to my nostrils; I could taste them on the air.

I visualised all the different scents dancing as they came together and separated again and again in different combinations and dosages. The shit was a bright green. Her sweat took on a dull yellow with her urine taking on dark vivid yellow of nightmares. My jiz was creamy white but that's a given.

I could nearly see the colours as they entered my body by way of my nostrils in different levels and combinations. I opened my mouth so I could taste the scents. It was relaxing and aided my recovery.

Twenty-four

I dozed off. I wasn't out for long. When I woke up I had recovered and was ready for the next round. My lovely wife had stopped her efforts to squirm away. Perhaps she had dozed off too.

I moved away. My intent was not to wake her. I didn't want her struggling until I held shit to her mouth (or already shoved it in). If she woke up and realised what I was doing there was a possibility of resistance. I didn't want that.

~MY DARLING WIFE~

I wish I didn't leave her with so much slack on the ankle chains. I checked the rope binding her wrists. Those seemed secure. But unfortunately she had the leverage of her flabby body to use against me.

I may have recovered but there was always a risk that she could suffocate me with her fat rolls which I found so sexy. I didn't want that to happen. Someone somewhere would miss us and report us missing. The police may break down the door and look in the basement and find us both dead (or she might even be barely alive dependent upon response time). The imagined headlines made me shudder. I didn't want anyone to find out my dirty little secret; I already had my eyes on another woman, one much younger than my lovely wife but lacking in a trachea ring, discovery could lead to my rejection.

She didn't move when I pulled down her pyjama bottoms and pants. She was still warm but I had to confirm she was still breathing. No matter what state she was in I thought she would have fought me off. She was always such a good submissive that it pissed me off but even I had thought I had gone too far this time.

I wrapped my arm over the front of her – flies moved away in my wake. Her pale white flesh felt sticky with humidity droplets and rampaging skin thrush. My fingers trailed through cooling jiz and flaking jiz from last night; that was much better to touch. I couldn't feel her breathing.

I snaked my hand under her flabby breast. Festering spores of mildew attached themselves to my clean skin. It was most unpleasant. I could feel them reproducing right away. I wanted to lick them off and savour them but checking on my lovely wife's breathing was more important.

Paranoia grew on my mind with threats to send me into a panicked frenzy. I couldn't feel her chest rise and fall. She couldn't be dead. Not yet. Not before I was ready.

Eternity stretched out before me. I could feel it digging into my mind in hateful taunts. My palms felt sweaty removing the fresh spores that would serve as a light meal while I was down here. Twinges of anger made me want to lash out at my lovely wife's unbreathing form. I managed to restrain myself; anger, or any intense emotion, would only result in me sweating more and losing more of my light meal.

It was just me and my lovely wife, flies buzzing all around us, in the black abyss. I wanted to suck the flies out of the air with my tongue but they moved too quickly for that. Besides, there were more important matters at hand – my lovely wife didn't seem to be breathing. I could eat flies whenever I wanted but I would only have one chance to fuck a trachea ring.

She was warm. She couldn't be dead. I needed her. If she had the nerve to die on me right now I would follow her into the afterlife and taunt her for eternity.

My chest tightened with a very visible belt of anxiety. I could practically see it caving in under the weight illuminated somehow in the perpetual darkness of the abyss.

My lungs struggled for stank humid air beneath the pressure. I couldn't manage an inhale. The belt tightened pulled by the buzzing flies. All because I thought my lovely wife might be dead.

I could feel my ribs cracking as the anxiety grew. I could hear them like ice. Everything went cold. Everything except my lovely wife, she was still warm.

My eyes bulged instead of my balls. They were coming out of their sockets to dangle on the membrane that connects them to the brain. It wasn't a very comfortable feeling. And my lovely wife wasn't in a position to soothe me.

I felt a light hammering beneath my hand. Maybe my lovely wife needed just the kiss of life before eating her own shit. Yes, that's it! Her heart was still beating. Her airways were probably blocked by something. Perhaps even a juicy maggot or two had hatched.

My eyes will go back in their sockets before they hang on by a thread and pull my brains out. The belt of anxiety will dissolve.

Then I remembered her trachea ring – the reason I married her in the first place. How the fuck do you give the kiss of life to someone with a trachea ring?

The belt tightened. My insides wanted to escape by way of my oesophagus; any lower and they would have burst out of my anus in a loud explosion. Everything was hopeless.

I pressed my sweaty palm flat beneath her soggy breast. The faint beating of her heart grew stronger but still no breath.

The first of my ribs broke, at least that is what it felt like – it was only later that I realised none of that actually happened. My lung was punctured and deflated like a balloon. The air escaped out of my side in a slow fart song. I didn't care about my lack of oxygen, I cared about my lovely wife's.

Flies buzzed, flying in a circle around us. The music they made was loud and ear shattering. It set my teeth on edge. More of them seemed to appear out of nowhere. It was like being caught in the centre of a tornado. My lovely wife's grey hair lifted in the fly-made wind. If she wasn't weighed down she might have blown away.

Our mattress floated in space. Even the flies seemed more distant. But I could still hear their buzz which threatened to send me to the mad house. I wanted to throw my hand over my ears but my lovely's wife sweaty flesh wanted to consume it and spit out the bones onto the mattress. I only had the one spare hand and that made the noise seem worse. I very nearly lost my balance. I wished for bug spray. Those bastards shouldn't have been tormenting me.

The blackness of the abyss threatened to swallow us (and the bastard flies to torment me forever). The air became cool. I didn't expect that. I thought it would have heated up and a giant snake would come out of the darkness and swallow us. I could actually hear the droplets of former humidity turn on ice on the mattress and creep closer to us. Unfortunately it didn't freeze the wings of the flies and make them drop out of the air. I wish it did.

I pulled my legs under me and curled my toes. I really thought there was ice. If I let it touch me then the frost bite would have been instant. It is really bizarre what one can think of while under intense stress.

The belt pulled tighter. I looked down and saw a swirl of yellow and grey as it stretched across my chest. The colours became more vivid as it became tighter.

Something seemed to exit my mouth. It felt like my throat, heart and lungs. It didn't feel very pleasant either. And certainly didn't taste nice.

I crossed my eyes and looked at my nose. Vivid red and black were seen but it was shapeless. Maybe it was essence of my insides rather than my actual insides. Either way, it fucking hurt.

While I was battling the tightening belt of anxiety squeezing my guts out of my mouth, my hand was pushed up. My lovely wife was breathing. I had never felt so relieved.

Everything happened with speed. The ice retreated. Essence of my insides found its proper home as the belt disappeared. She was alive. It was such a relief that I nearly had a panic attack in the immediate come-down of anxiety.

Twenty-five

I went back to gathering a giant turd to serve her for dinner. When her time comes, she'll die admitting she doesn't shit roses. I'll make sure she knows it came from her.

~MY DARLING WIFE~

Alive, yes, but she was out cold. I planned on waking her once the shit was in her mouth. Her unconsciousness made it easier. There wasn't any struggle.

I reached my hand into her pyjama bottoms in search of the dry crusty shit that smelt nowhere near as bad as her farts (maybe it did when it was fresh but I wasn't there when the function was carried out). I was careful not to let its crusty outsides fool me. I knew that if I squeezed down I would break the crust and my hand would be covered in it.

Warm air exited her arse onto my hand. I wasn't too happy about that. It took a moment for the smell to catch up to my nose. She had obviously emptied her bowels. I don't get how it still smelt that bad. Like month old boiled eggs left to decompose side by side with mouldy festering king prawns down the sides of a piss-stained sofa.

I pulled my hand away before she could fart again. My fist loosely held onto the giant piece of shit. I had never before seen her shit. Whenever she used the toilet she made sure it all went down and cleaned it afterwards.

My lovely wife was still out cold. She was one to sleep with her mouth open so I knew that wouldn't be an issue. That's probably how she ended needing a trachea ring in the first place, swallowed down too many poisonous spiders in her sleep. I never asked her about it. I didn't care. The important thing was that she had one.

I pulled myself up by grabbing onto her flab. My nails dug in. I could feel skin and flesh beneath them. My other hand balanced the giant piece of shit. After my momentous orgasm it was a difficult task. My bones creaked and my muscles were stiff. She failed to wake.

As expected her mouth was wide open, her flat yellow teeth on display even as she lay on her side with her tongue hanging out. I shoved the turd into her mouth.

Twenty-six

Now I needed to wake her. I needed her to know what she was swallowing. I needed her fully conscious to achieve that. I was more than tempted to run upstairs for her electronic voice box so she could offer feedback on the experience but I didn't, I wanted the instant gratification of 'now' and running upstairs to search it out would result in too much of a delay for my liking.

There's nothing better than surprise sex from behind – unless you put it in the wrong hole. She needed to be woken up like that just once. She was an anal virgin, emphasis on the 'was'.

I knew I wouldn't cum so soon after ejaculating in a giant, mind-numbing orgasm but I did have a massive throbbing erection. It was going to be a tight squeeze. I could barely get my finger in there.

My lovely wife failed to wake up. I wanted to roll her onto her front as that would've made it easier to stick my cock into her anus. But I didn't want her shit to fall out of her open mouth. I would have to push past her arse fat and fuck her on my side. I'm fit; I knew I could handle it.

I moved my finger around in circles trying to stretch her arsehole enough to fit my cock without cutting off circulation. She didn't wake. I added in another finger. My cock is fairly wide – an entire three inches and a bit, I've measured it with the tape measure from her sewing kit. I was sure to wipe dick-cheese on it before putting it away so whatever she next measured would have a little bit of me on it.

I eased my cock in. The tightness of her anus pushed down. I wished for some lubricant. My foreskin was pulled back uncomfortably. I thought it might be ripped off. But it was worth it.

She moved. I must have been waking her. My lovely wife's arsehole must have felt like it was on fire. The fire would have burned through her sending the signals to wake the fuck up and swallow what was in her mouth – her shit.

If her arse would start bleeding then the blood could act as a lube. If she would have diarrhoea then I would really win my 'you shit' argument and had a lubricant while stealing her anal virginity. But I'm not that lucky.

I began to thrust in and out. Slowly at first because it was such a tight squeeze. I soon gained speed as my wide cock stretched her brown hole. Shit that she failed to expel and that I failed to wipe with my hand attached itself to me.

I don't know if my lovely wife realised what was happening. I doubt that she did. Not upon waking. She was always so disorientated for the first few minutes of the morning.

She was moving though. Maybe she was trying to escape a burning that she thought was diarrhoea. If only it actually was. But I was never that lucky to begin with.

I didn't hear chewing. But I didn't hear spitting either. I would have to assume the giant turd, her giant turd, was still in her mouth. I wanted to watch her eat it and make sure she swallows it all. I wanted to wipe her chin with my fingers and make her suck on them. Which is exactly what I did.

The springs in the mattress creaked as I gained speed. Circulation no longer cut off to my dick as her virginal arsehole stretched out further. I tried to push in deeper. I know I had ejaculated once already but I thought I might cum again.

I grabbed her shoulder with one hand and her lank greying locks with the other. I wanted to leave a bruise and pull out some hair. I wrapped the greying course strands through my hand and pulled. Her neck cracked back. I didn't want to break it – that could kill her before her time. She struggled to get her neck facing the correct direction. I allowed it but I wouldn't allow her anus to escape my cock. I didn't hear any spitting noises. Maybe she failed to notice the shit in her mouth. Maybe she wasn't fully awake and aware yet. I was sure to inform her once I had finished and was glaring at her with post orgasm face.

A fresh orgasm built in my balls. It wasn't going to be as big as the one I had a few minutes previous. I banged her arsehole with increased speed. I freed her hair as I didn't want to risk her neck. I could feel it. I knew then for a fact that I could suck my jiz out of her arse if I so desired (which I did, once I recovered and she ate her shit).

Without her plastic voice box she couldn't speak. I was tempted to give it to her to hear her complaints but I didn't want my lovely wife altering the neighbours to her predicament. I didn't want to run upstairs to get it either. I wanted to stay with her.

Twenty-seven

I pulled out of her arse. I wasn't as wasted as I was immediately following the previous rain of cum. I pushed her onto her back aided with the strength of adrenaline. I straddled her. I could feel her trying to roll back onto her side as I held her down with my legs (as soon as I left her she went back onto her side, some sort of reflex, I think). I wanted to watch the shit fall down her throat without putting her on her back because I had intentions of swallowing my jiz (wish I had bought a straw with me but I didn't know where they were kept).

I leaned forward. Pulverised shit leaked out of her mouth. I reached up and wiped it off. I shoved my finger into her full mouth. I don't think my lovely wife was aware of it. It was a pity so I pinched her cheeks with my free hand. When that failed to revive her enough to swallow I twisted her nipple. She didn't like that. It probably reminded her of what it felt like to have my cock up her arse. She swallowed without sound.

The look of revulsion was clear on her face. She looked like she had aged by hundred years. It turned me on all over again. I wish I could fuck her skeleton. Eye sockets and a nose cavity and that's just on her skull. The possibilities of bone sex remained endless. I could even shove her thigh bone up my arse while I jerk off.

I saw what I wanted and rolled off her before I came too carried away with my fantasy and killed her without first fucking her trachea ring. That's all I really wanted, her beautiful trachea ring.

She promptly rolled back onto her side. The mattress creaked its disagreement.

A straw would have made sucking my jiz out of her arse easier but I didn't have one so I had to make do with my tongue. I was sure that the sensation of my warm, rough tongue would be more uncomfortable for her than shoving a straw up her freshly deflowered arsehole. My nose was pressed up against her arsecrack, I was certain she noticed but was in too much of shock to squirm away or roll onto her back.

Residue of my lovely wife's shit greeted my taste buds and mated with my salty creamy white. The sauce was rich yet thin due to my previous ejaculation. I wished the earlier one was in her arse – it would be turdballs in gravy, a pleasant dinner party idea.

I decided that instead of swallowing, I would share with my lovely wife. She deserved some too, like a weird and twisted snowball.

I leaned over and spat in her mouth with her still on her side. Her eyes flickered open on impact. The taste was strong but I doubt it overpowered the shit. She should have appreciated that I was washing her mouth out. She should swallow but I wasn't that concerned about it. She had her meal, I didn't care if she had the drink or not.

I went back to foraging in her butt with my tongue. She put in no effort to stop me. I was confident that she knew what was happening and that I was going to spit into her mouth again. Maybe she resigned herself to punishment by this point. Maybe she even thought that if she was obedient that I would let her escape with her life. But there was never any chance of that.

Shit coated her flat yellow teeth. Semen from my previous visit stared back at me. My lovely wife hadn't even bothered to shut her mouth. I spat again.

I held her mouth shut and massaged the underside of her chin. Liquidified shit that she failed to swallow leaked out. I couldn't see my semen in the shit deluge. I'm surprised she disobeyed me so thoroughly. I know some of it landed in her stomach to be shat out tonight or tomorrow. I once again found myself wiping her face with my fingers and forcing them into her mouth. She didn't bite me. She wasn't rewarded for withholding her teeth.

Obviously she was denied usage of a toothbrush. I wasn't sure if she remembered their existence. Or of toothpaste, dental floss and mouthwash. I reminded her of what she was missing. The expression on her face was so priceless I wished for my camera to preserve it forever.

After her ordeal I was kind enough to inform her she had just ate her own shit seasoned with the salty creamy white that is my cum. I made sure she understood the shit was her own. She mouthed something but never did bother to learn to read her lips. Maybe sound came out but my ears weren't that sharp. She looked disgusted.

It was a first for her, swallowing my cum. It was probably the first time she had swallowed anyone's jiz. And having to acknowledge a bodily function that she so often denied all in the same day. It must have blown her mind. I'm surprised she didn't faint.

She looked like she wanted to vomit but I told her she would be lapping that up too if she did. I so much wanted for her to be sick though. That way I could have held the back of her neck while I forced her to lick the festering mattress.

Twenty-eight

I left her to struggle while I put up the fly paper. I didn't hear any retching or any spitting. It rather disappointed me.

It was nice hearing her chains jingle. I whistled along while keeping me ears tuned for the sound of my lovely wife trying to eliminate the taste from her mouth. They never arrived.

Once I was done I watched her a few minutes before injecting her with heroin. She stared at me with an expression that begged release. She would have the ultimate release, but not yet. She received temporary release but that was only so she couldn't escape and alert the neighbours.

I gave her a kiss on the cheek and went upstairs to shower and head out for an evening of cheap hookers and diseases. I wasn't sure if the diseases would offer a short enough incubation period to ensure that my lovely wife became infected before she died. I supposed it didn't really matter.

Twenty-nine

Everything is nearly ready. Now that the moment is so close I feel oddly calm and collected. I thought I would be anxious with large butterflies floating around in my stomach trying to induce vomiting of stomach bile. But they aren't there. I haven't even broken into a sweat, yet.

There are less flies about. A lot of them met a slow demise on the fly paper. I might be able to pick off the half dead ones and eat them. They might come apart in my fingers but that doesn't matter. The noise is less intimidating.

I haven't needed to drug my lovely wife in over a day. Her body is starting to break down. I wish there was a way to ensure that she would be aware of what was going to happen to her, but I couldn't think of one.

I walked down the stairs. They groaned beneath my weight. I wondered if my lovely wife could hear them as they threatened to decompose and break one or both of my ankles. Maybe she took in the noise and processed it somewhere in her delirious mind into something else. Something worse than her second husband walking down some stairs. I liked that thought.

I put on shoes and socks before I walked down the stairs. I didn't put on anything else – there was no point. I didn't want to feel the dirty concrete on my feet or risk a splinter on the wooden stairs. They were heavy steel-toe shoes incase I wanted to kick my lovely wife after I fucked her dying breath away.

I reached the bottom of the stairs. Everything was gloomy and the humidity threatened to send me back up. It was like it wanted to protect my lovely wife from her fate or delay it a bit longer so she could die in peace.

Her mattress was cast in shadow. I couldn't see my lovely wife but I could smell her. The worms and the maggots were doing their jobs in aiding her decomposition. My stomach sunk a little at the thought; what if she had died down here all alone and without my cock fucking away her dying breath through her trachea ring.

A cloud of putrid decay took the Humidity Express to my nose. I inhaled deeply. I wanted to wallow in it. I paused a moment so I could feel the smell enter my pores and then my blood stream.

A few flies buzzed towards me. They probably wanted revenge for the agonising deaths of their relatives. I batted them away. They were too fast for me to catch and eat otherwise I would've picked them out of the air one by one and had a little snack. I wished I had a tongue like a frog; frogs have fast tongues. I still wish I had a tongue like a frog.

The air was oppressive and only stirred by the few buzzing flies that didn't meet with a slow death on the fly paper. None landed on me. They were more interested in her. They have grown fat on my lovely wife and her festering mattress. They only wanted to stop me from wallowing in delicious putrid odours and maybe get a little revenge for their relatives.

I'm grateful that no wasps have found their way down here. The last thing I want is my cock swelling due to a painful sting rather than anticipation. Vengeful wasps wouldn't be very pleasant at all. My cock already had one date with wasps. Once was enough. This was a separate fantasy turned into reality. I could only carry out all my fantasies together in my dreams.

I wished I ordered some Viagra from the internet – that could have prolonged my erection and delayed ejaculation. But it was too late. Another few hours and my lovely wife would be dead. Even if I could have got it from the chemist, I wouldn't have the time.

Thirty

I walked over to her. Blood pumped into my cock. With a throbbing erection I became light headed. My lovely wife didn't move in the shadows. I couldn't hear the springs on her mattress.

I didn't think my wife was aware of my presence. It was time to make her aware. If I wasn't so erect, I would make her aware by pissing on her.

Beneath the flies and their offspring she still wore a few scraps of clothing. I wished I had brought scissors down. That way, for the first time in her adult life she could be completely naked with nothing to cover herself up with. But I didn't have scissors.

Worms didn't burrow through her skin, at least from what I was able to see. I wasn't sure if they would or not when I put them on the bare mattress. I didn't get a close inspection of her body before returning upstairs and nailing the basement door shut and covering it with tiles later in the week.

I was hoping that when I got in close I might discover one coming out of her ear and another out of her nose. Sadly, it didn't happen. If they were there I would have sucked them out and swallowed.

It looks like she might have developed a bed sore or two. Or maybe those are worm holes, like in freshly picked apples straight from the orchard. Not worm holes to travel to a different dimension, although that would be wonderful – especially if there was one where all woman had trachea rings.

I couldn't tell in the gloom. I needed to know. Bed sores may not be as great as a dimension where all women had trachea rings but they could prove to be fun and painful (for her). Even up close I couldn't tell. I required more light.

I wish I replaced the other light bulbs down here. Her late and great husband installed three lights; I only put a fresh bulb in one. If I had thought ahead there would be light bulbs in all of them and a cupboard filled with little treats for my wife – like a flexible straw catheter so she could drink her own urine.

Now I need to go upstairs to fetch a torch. If I had thought ahead I wouldn't have needed one except to closely inspect her anus and it would already be in the cupboard. But I didn't think ahead. I'm useless at stuff like that unless it involves my own direct pleasure (such as worms and flies). She should have thought of it. She was always thinking ahead.

Three days ago I had the foresight to shut all the curtains and keep them shut so the neighbours wouldn't be suspicious that I'm wandering around my house wearing only shoes and socks. Although they might be suspicious that I haven't opened them in days and they haven't seen my lovely wife in equally as long.

I reached into the pantry. On the top shelf where my lovely wife never dusted sits various household items. I found the torch by feel lurking behind something without a dusty description. I knocked over a dish of nails and screws in the process and stirred around a vast amount of dust. I probably disturbed more than one spider. I never had a need to go up there but if I had known about all the dust I would have said something to her about it and worn her down until she did something.

I wanted so badly to get back to my lovely wife and her possible bedsores as quickly as possible. It was tempting to take the stairs two at a time as I sometimes took my hookers but I didn't want to risk my neck especially before I fucked the life out of her.

I hoped so much that those marks I saw were bedsores and not shadows cast by her decomposing cellulite. I made plans to wake my lovely wife by fucking them. I couldn't say putting my dick in a bedsore was a bucket list item but when the opportunity strikes it would be pointless to waste it and regret it forever.

I hadn't fed her in days – it seemed pointless. Besides, she could have eaten her shit if she was really that hungry. I'm sure the aftertaste of that giant turd I served her a few days previous still graced her mouth.

I clicked the torch on. It appeared that she wasn't that hungry after all. Her stomach and intestines must have been completely empty by this point. Later that week I would murder a prostitute to find out if it is true that the last thing people do when they die is shit because my lovely wife was empty. Really empty. Even that shit I made her eat must had passed through her by that point.

I knelt on the mattress next to her. It squeaked as I rested my weight upon it. I'm surprised the springs hadn't rusted into dust. My lovely wife continued her probable blank eyed examination of the wall. Well, she might have been in a deep sleep. I couldn't see her eyes.

I brushed maggots off her shoulder. My cock was nice and hard. I had been waiting for this moment my entire life – or at least since I started being plagued by wet dreams. I wanted to prolong it and make it stretch forever.

A shy worm squirmed under her and away from the light of my torch. I planned to get it once I flipped her over to inspect those bedsores – it would be a nice tasty morsel. But first I wanted to caress my lovely wife.

Thirty-one

The springs from the soiled mattress poked my toned arse as I took a seat next to her. An odour of mildew mixed with piss, shit and sweat puffed up my nose in a great cloud. I inhaled deeply enjoying the way the scent tasted and the way the mattress springs dug into me. I like a bit of pain mixed with my pleasure.

She really was beautiful, even covered in the decaying fragments of her pyjamas and flakes of jiz and shit. My lovely wife was the most beautiful woman on the planet. It was all down to her trachea ring. Although the way she laid there defenceless made my heart swell but not as much as my cock.

Her pyjama bottoms were pulled down, her shit caked arse on display. I grabbed it with such a force that I broke one of my nails. I wanted to dig in further but I didn't want to risk any more of my nails.

I forced my finger into her anus loosened by surprise anal sex from behind. She failed to move, which was disappointing. I needed her to be aware of me. I wanted to watch her eyes as I fucked away her life.

She probably no longer felt just one finger. So I added another. She didn't feel that one either.

I caressed her depleted stomach with my other hand. It is amazing what a few days of starvation can achieve. I even think she had a bit of extra skin that wasn't there when I brought her down here. I pulled on it letting her thrush infection experience humid air and artificial light. She still had fat too but not as much.

I continued to examine her anus with my two exploring fingers. I thought I should fist her – if it would fit. That should have woken her.

I didn't want to risk losing my fist in her anus. I didn't want to take any chances on her last night.

Vaseline would have been useful. As I've already mentioned, my ability to plan ahead was near enough non-existent so I didn't have a little cupboard filled with useful little things. But there was some Vaseline in the bathroom cabinet. The thirty or so seconds required to fetch it wouldn't make any difference at all. I wished I thought of getting it when I went to get the torch.

I went upstairs and fetched the Vaseline out of the bathroom. I wondered how many more trips the wooden stairs had left in them. Not too many. I knew that. I didn't want to be trapped away from my lovely wife and I didn't want to break my ankle should they collapse while I was on them.

I wondered if there was anything else I should get while I was up there. Probably. But I couldn't think of anything. I couldn't think of anything until I actually needed it, one of my flaws I'm afraid.

I stopped in the kitchen for spare batteries for my torch on my way to the basement. They were kept in a dust free drawer. I looked around to see if anything else would jump to the top of my mind. There wasn't. I turned around to see if that would help.

I walked down the stairs into the gloom and humidity. I'm surprised the moisture hadn't caused them to decay. I wished my lovely wife's late and great first husband had the foresight to install a banister to take some of my weight. Or, better yet, new concrete stairs. But I don't think he was that intelligent.

I took my seat on the mattress. It squeaked its approval and sent up a cloud of dried mould with highlights of shit and jiz flakes. A spring tried to find its way into my anus but that way was blocked. I paid for a tetanus injection when I found the mattress at the side of the road, just in case.

Thirty-two

I opened the Vaseline. The lid was greasy but I didn't mind, my hand up to my wrist was about to become greasy. I smoothed my hand in the yellow goo and then applied some up to my wrist. The seal was probably water tight but I didn't have a tap to test the theory. However I did have humidity. Beads of water droplets clung to the Vaseline but didn't seem to penetrate. The role of keeping my hand moist was taken up by sweat.

I planned to roll her over by using the fist I was about to force into her anus. It might wake her up. I hoped it would wake her up. I wanted her to be in delirious pain.

Then I planned to inspect her possible bed sores. I really hoped they were bedsores. I wanted to stick my dick in them and make her mouth curl into a squeal of pain she would never be able to vocalise.

I pried apart her arsecheeks. Maggots glistened at me in a warm greeting. They were my friends even though I participated in population control and ate some of them. But they didn't mind, not really.

I clicked off the torch. I didn't mind fisting her in the gloom. I liked the way the shadows cast from the bare light bulb played on her sagging curves and extra skin. I poked it to watch them wobble. The torch hit the dirty floor. I noticed because the sound wasn't as I thought it would be. Instead it was muffled by something that I can only assume was mould or a patch of toadstools.

With my lubricated hand I inserted three fingers through dried shit with ease. I twirled them around a bit to stretch her anus ready for my large fist. The remaining flies buzzed their encouragement. Her arsehole was inviting and probably dry but I wouldn't know due to the coating of Vaseline.

I pulled out with a pop that I hope she heard. Air followed me out but I think that was air I pushed into her rather than her toxic farts. The smell that greeted my nose was no worse than the mildew scent with highlights of shit, piss and jiz that surrounded me and burrowed into my pores.

I punched her anus. Resistance said hello. I didn't expect it considering the thick coating of Vaseline but I guess her arsehole didn't fancy having my fist shoved into it. I don't think my lovely wife was capable of clenching her arse at that point.

I pushed my fist in further. It was like saying 'fuck you' to her for all those times she wouldn't have regular vanilla missionary sex with me. I wanted to say the words but I didn't want the neighbours to hear. I wanted to say them because of all the times she wouldn't be adventurous.

With sudden delight her anus wanted to suck my fist in and crush the bones with all the pressure. It probably realised it could use it for nourishment. Even unconscious, my lovely wife was hungry. I find it sweet that her arse was trying to suck all the flesh from my bones. It was very like her.

I went with it. At that point it didn't matter if my hand broke. I had a great story about fisting a man I just met at the pub to tell the nurse at A and E just in case the situation arose. It didn't but there are some things that are good to prepare for – some ways my brain has rare foresight.

My lovely wife's anus swallowed my fist up to my wrist. I lost circulation. It was like my fist had been sucked into a black hole. It wasn't the most comfortable feeling in the world but it was worth it. I had fisted plenty of cheap drug addicted hookers, both anally and vaginally and one let me stick a fist in each hole at the same time, but I had never fisted my lovely wife or a long term girlfriend; they were all too prude. A fly landed on my elbow.

I hoped that wherever my lovely wife's consciousness was hiding it was able to feel my fist. The fly stared at me even as I shook my arm to ensure that somewhere deep inside she was able to feel it to the point of tasting it (and tasting fresh shit in the back of her throat).

Thirty-three

The arm stuck in her backside made rolling over her obese mass much easier. I was able to push with my spare arm and put extra weight inside of her.

I leant down to kiss her arse and ended up inhaling a maggot – an added bonus. It was an accident, of course. I enjoyed the surprise of it. I looked for more in the gloom, glistening bits of white in the darkness. Eating them would give me strength. They were gifts from my friends the remaining flies.

When I wanted more maggots there weren't any but I saw the end (or beginning) of a juicy pink worm. It went down like a moving piece of bloated spaghetti. I should have cut it in half. Maggots were plentiful. Worms weren't so plentiful. There were only the ones I brought from the shop. I didn't know the mechanics of worm reproduction (and still don't) but I didn't think a few days was enough to create more big juicy ones.

I put my free hand under her. The mattress creaked at me and threatened me by stabbing me with more rusty old springs. It was no deterrent. Nothing was going to ruin my special moment. After all, I had lived my life to fuck someone's trachea ring.

My lovely's wife flesh was hot like she had a fever and it felt broken and cracked while still being moist. I assumed what I felt were bed sores but I wouldn't know for certain until I flipped her all the way over.

Her anus continued its grinding consumption of my fist. The pain was worth it. In my deepest dreams I live it over again and again. I think, somewhere buried inside me, is a secret masochist who only comes out at night.

Even after starvation she was very heavy and curvy. In fact, I would argue that starvation made her worse. Her deflated rolls had a weight that only extra skin could give them. I needed to trick them to fall on the other side of my lovely wife to aide in turning her over.

My hand was sucked further up her arse. It wanted my wrist flesh next to feed her rolls and inflate them once again. If I had any close friends I might have discussed my theories on the situation with them. But I had no one and my parents especially disgusted me.

I succeeded in rolling over my lovely wife and her deflated rolls. I needed to check her trachea ring. The trachea ring, and the trachea ring alone, was the reason I was interested in her in the first place. I couldn't have that blocked and have her die before I fucked away her dying breath.

Fucking her corpse just didn't have the appeal that her trachea ring did.

Thirty-four

Before I could examine her bedsores and articulate why wanted her in the first place, I unfortunately needed to remove my fist. This was much easier to think about than actually do.

The suction was intense. I swear her arsehole was in league with her deflated fat rolls to suck me up and consume me completely. I don't even think it would have spat out my bones. They were too tasty and contained too many vitamins that her fat could use to sustain itself that little bit longer.

I reached over and pulled with my other arm. My hand was sucked into her fat. It wanted that one as well. With grave risk to my feet, I stood up on her and pulled with every ounce of me. My shoes sunk into her flesh. When I was able to pull them away, they were coated with a furry white layer that just wouldn't come off so I had to bury them in a landfill. I wanted to keep them as a memento of my special evening alone with my lovely wife. I'll always have the memories though; nothing can take them away from me.

Flipping my lovely wife over onto her back was much easier than trying to convince her arsehole to let me have my hand back. I found it surprising that her anus didn't have teeth. I suppose old people, children and drug addicts can gum their food though.

I pulled with all my body's worth of strength. My shoes sunk into her arse-fat. They were real leather. I'm sure her blubber saw that as food. Then the cotton-blend socks; those might be edible in a pinch. Maybe denying her food wasn't such a good idea. Her body seemed set on consuming me. It was like quicksand with super-mutant fast-acting flesh eating bacteria. Given the chance, I'm sure my bones would have been eaten too.

The humidity pressed down upon me like a trip to the deep sea. At least there were air pockets though, otherwise I would have drowned before living my life's only purpose. I would have come back to haunt anyone and everyone with a trachea ring and have ghost sex with them.

I couldn't maintain my erection. The oppressive air wouldn't allow it. I didn't need my erection while I was wrist deep in her anus and my shoes were being dissolved by her flesh-eating arsecheeks but I wanted to be able to keep it up.

A great droning buzzing reached my ears. The air was stirred by something out of my range of vision. My fist was blocking her anus; I was able to conclude that it wasn't the odour-less arse-gas that she seldom released. Plus her arse never droned. It sounded like a wasp, or many wasps and hornets, together. I knew there wasn't one wasp in the basement, let alone a swarm. I was careful to keep my home wasp-free as of late.

I looked around, even though it hurt to move my neck due to the intensive grinding air pressure. All I could see were flies. Fucking flies everywhere. None of them had even the faintest hint of yellow. I didn't believe that flies could make that much racket, even if they were angry due to the premature sticky deaths of their loved ones.

But the droning buzz became louder and more intense as I sunk further into her arse-fat. This wasn't right. This wasn't meant to happen. Everything should run smoothly for me at all times. Flies couldn't be the cause of that much noise.

The air filled with electricity. I could nearly hear it crackling like a mad old witch but I could have imagined that. Air pressure combined with stress can result in some bizarre hallucinations and even temporary psychosis.

All my body hair stood on end as my arm was sucked further into my lovely wife's arse. It was up to the elbow at that point. I didn't think that was possible but I suppose I had seen films from Mexico with woman taking anal from a horse. But my lovely wife was no porn star.

Sweat dripped from my nude body in my struggles to free myself. I didn't seem to have any cotton blend socks left to absorb it. Her super-mutant flesh eating bacteria had consumed them along with my shoes. I could feel it eating into my feet. It wanted my dignity next but that was never going to happen, not to a man like me.

I tried moving around my hand inside her. There was actually a lot of space. My brain wanted to explode with confusion. Her gapping anus hand plenty of room but wouldn't let me go. It didn't have any teeth to use to bite down and grip. There was no reason why it should have continued to hold me hostage.

I opened my fist and tried to scratch. It made no difference. I could feel flakes of her inner anus beneath my nails and still, it wouldn't release my arm. The flakes actually seemed to make the problem worse. The anal flakes beneath my nails forced them to peel back in an effort to fuse my hand to her anal wall.

~MY DARLING WIFE~

The coating of Vaseline was long dissolved and consumed by her starving body so I had no protection. I wish I had thought to purchase veterinary gloves. They would be like wearing a condom on my fist, although, on second thoughts, her arse would have probably eaten through them as well, even if I doubled up.

It was like it had a mind of its own, completely independent from my unconscious lovely wife. I was beginning to suspect that might be the case at least. Her body did have a sense of fight or flight for survival but years of submission had bred it out of her conscious form and deep into her subconscious where it would only come out if she was desperate and totally unaware of it.

Something razor sharp dug into my wrist. I think it was at that point that her anus developed teeth. As if my inner thoughts of anal teeth resulted in them. I could feel the warm beads of blood separate from her warm arsehole. Maybe the blood, my blood, would serve as a lubricant to replace the lost Vaseline so I could free myself.

Flies landed on me, possibly looking for somewhere to lay more eggs while I was defenceless. They could have landed on her and left their next generation in her, where they belonged. Not on me. I didn't deserve it. I gave them life. These were the best of the best flies, the ones that were smart enough to not land on the fly paper. They should have been smart enough to not land on me.

My lovely wife failed to wake up while I struggled to free my arm. I hope that somewhere in the back of her mind she was aware of the immense pain her physical body was in. I hope her brain was screaming in sheer agony due to my struggles.

Her anus finally decided to release me. It was a violent way to gain freedom. I wanted a gentle discharge from prison that was her arse. My lovely wife's unconscious fight or flight response made sure I received punishment for imagined wrongs.

I fell backwards and hit the wall. The mould that grew on it tried to trap me there; a conspiracy so her anus could get revenge for my failed efforts to bring it pleasure. My lovely wife's unconscious form was in league with everything in that basement. I don't see why. If I died down there then there would have been no possibility of escape for her.

An examination with two mirrors sometime later would reveal terrible bruising and a need to fill the bath with cold water and ice cubes. If my lovely wife wasn't dead and I wasn't so sore and stiff I would have killed her again. Oh how

I wished it were possible to bring people back from the afterlife just to torture and kill her each and every day.

Thirty-five

Flies landed on my lovely wife's bedsores. The conspiracy against me seemed to have ceased at that point. The basement was probably more than aware that I was about to lose what little control I had over my temper.

I knelt on the mattress, the springs sighed their rusty greetings. I leant in for a close examination of her bedsores and clicked the torch back on. The smell they emitted was less than pleasant but I wanted to bottle it as a perfume for when I visit cheap hookers.

I poked with my index finger on my hand that was already beginning to swell. Pus didn't ooze out — it squirted like female ejaculation. I caught some in my hand and licked. It offered a type of nourishment that maggots couldn't.

I fingered in preparation of sticking my cock in. My fist was still too traumatised to go exploring as a whole. I would soon make one lucky bedsore considerably larger with my stiff cock. At least, that was the plan.

I didn't realise sticking my dick in a festering pus-filled bedsore would burn so much. I had to pull out right away. I might have risked it but a cock injury could have prevented me from fucking her dying breath out of her – I didn't think she had another few hours in her, let alone the time it would take me to recover. Especially if her pus ate through my penis skin and made it bleed.

The maggots glistened out of the shadows cast by her curves during my recovery. I wiped my erection with my bare hand to remove all the burning pus. I removed my shoes, which were miraculously intact following their ordeal in her arse-fat, to get to my cotton blend socks. I used a sock to wipe it all away until the burning ceased.

Thirty-six

I picked up a lonely maggot between my thumb and index finger. It tried to squirm away. I was careful not to squish it as I raised it to my lips and swallow like taking a pill but this is a different type of high. I looked for another. Maggots were plentiful. A few in my tummy wouldn't impact the overall dream.

I needed to recover my strength – fisting and bedsores was rather traumatising. I sat on the edge of the mouldy mattress and plucked maggots from her. I was tempted to chew but they went down easier swallowed. Besides I didn't like the idea of a maggot bursting between my teeth. I needed to mentally prepare for carrying out my life's work.

I swallowed another maggot. I needed to roll my lovely wife back over so I could get at her throat. On her back would be the easiest. And I would be able to look down and watch her face as life left her.

I set about the task in the gloom. Her fat and the festering mattress seemed to have merged into one in the short time she was face down. Her clammy skin served as a glue of sorts.

With my recent and unfair injuries it was tough going but my entire life had been lived leading up to making love to someone's trachea ring. Sweat dripped from me and fed her super-mutant flesh eating bacteria and skin-wide thrush infection lurking deep in her fat rolls.

My body was kind enough to release extra adrenaline. It coursed through my veins making sure I received the extra strength required to get my lovely wife's bulbous mass onto her back.

Her breathing was shallow and she was feverish. The heat from her wanted to push me away in her body's last ditch effort to fight me off. Her glassy eyes were open – soon she'd be staring at the ceiling. I snapped my fingers in front of her. I was disappointed by the lack of response.

My lovely wife's end was near. And I had no idea what I would do with my life after this point.

I pulled on her orange peel arm. The flesh was dimple pocked down to the bone due to her recent starvation. The super-mutant flesh eating bacteria would never consume my lovely wife or her not so lovely skin-wide thrush infection.

With her halfway over I climbed without letting go of her arm and shoved my knees into her bloated belly to push the rest of the way. The mattress didn't want to release her skin and fat. I could hear the skin tearing away from it. To this day, I'm still not sure which one was consuming which.

Worms slithered to the complete festering darkness beneath her. It was amazing she didn't crush them but I suppose fat is more absorbent than muscle. And there was space inside her bedsores and anus for them to make a home.

My thighs sunk into her stomach like it was trying to eat me. I didn't want to go there. Not again. Not after my feet were so recently nearly consumed. But there was no other way. I wanted to watch her face as I stuck my cock in. I had escaped her flesh once, I could do it again.

Thirty-seven

Her arse released decayed putrid gas clouds. For once, it wasn't a turn off. Blood pumped to my cock. I thought it might throb too hard and explode. I stuck my finger into the hole in her neck. It welcomed me. It was like that lovely little hole on my lovely wife's neck knew what it was there for.

I stuck my tongue in. The taste was exquisite and like nothing I had ever had before (or since). The salt from her sweat met with the sweet bread dough taste of thrush harboured all over her fat rolls. I didn't want to let it go but I knew my lovely wife didn't have much time left.

A long stream of pre-ejaculation escaped my cock. I was close to bursting. I didn't want to ruin it. My entire life would have been rendered worthless. After all this anticipation and preparation I shoved my cock in without ceremony.

The feeling was all I imagined it to be and more as I pushed in and out of her. The flies buzzed around. The rusty springs creaked. For a fraction of a moment, my lovely wife's pupils dilated – she was aware. I blew my load into her neck as her eyes returned to their glassy stare and she ceased the struggle to breath.

Satisfaction never felt so good. I gave her a final kiss on her dead lips as I recovered and stroked her greying locks that one last time. I dozed off a little bit; at least, I think I did. When strength returned, I stood up and went up the stairs. They didn't collapse. I never looked back at her festering form on the decaying mattress.

END.

TOENAILS

By Dani Brown

ONE

Upon waking, the first thing to be considered before even the coffee was put on, was how to score enough toenails to see me through the day. They were like crack to me; only more addictive and typically not as foul smelling.

Some people need coffee to get going in the mornings. Others need smack to chase night demons out of their veins. I required toenail clippings, swallowed down with a glass of tap water. Coffee was only second – the bitter brown with Snow White and the Seven Cubes gulped down to make me normal in appearance only.

I did not enjoy sucking or chewing on the precious toenails until later in the day. In an ideal world I would have ample supplies of toenails to swallow down like pills no matter what time it was. But some mornings I had to start by chewing. That was often the case these days. Toenail supplies were becoming shorter by the day.

Next to my bed, resting on the table, I kept an ashtray. It was meant to contain toenails but its usual state these past few months had been one of complete emptiness. Not even the dust of toenails was contained in it. A despairing sight, enough to send me plunging to the depths of clinical depression. Prozac could not cure my need for toenails.

I needed a full ashtray encase I woke in the night with a bad case of the nibbles. Cravings would keep deep sleep forever out of my reach. Prozac did not help in that matter either. In fact, I was beginning to believe Prozac was a pill of exceptional uselessness.

My wife's toenails were clipped away. I made her apply special paint three times a day to keep her in a state of permanent nail infection –they were stronger that way and hit my blood with more speed than an injection of diamorphine. But she needed toenails for it to actually work. My addiction kept them trimmed down to the cuticle.

The baby, I could chew on his toenails without clipping them. In fact, such behaviour was encouraged by the health visitor. Despite his regularly increasing sizes of clothing, his toenails did not grow quick enough to satisfy me.

It would be seen as cruel (and noticeable to that damn cock-sucking health visitor) to give my baby son a fungal nail infection but in the darkest hour, when the moon had set and the sun had yet to rise, I would sneak into the bedrooms of the other two and apply two coats of my wife's special paint. She was aware of what I was doing – powerless to stop it. Some credit is due my intense hen-pecking of her; she was too emotionally beaten down to protect her snotnose brats.

I was God's gift, or so I had managed to convince her. God's gift of what, she never enquired. Maybe God's gift of toenails? She would never be capable of surviving without me anyways. Submissive and emotionally beaten, that was how I liked her. The only love I had to spare was for toenails.

Sometimes, I wished for her to transform into a man. When I could not source enough toenails for satisfaction, dick cheese was an acceptable offering to the gods of withdrawal. I did not know whether, in the fundamentals of sex change operations, female-to-male transition resulted in the cheese of the gods though. If I snapped my fingers, she would go through with it to please me.

My ashtray was empty. Not even the ghosts of toenails lingered. It was a state I did not much appreciate waking up to. Before shaking could take over, I ran a finger into my foreskin – dry, always so fucking dry.

My wife snored next to me, oblivious to my predicament in the warm arms of her dreams. Sleep was the only escape she had. I was kind enough to allow it provided she kept her feet wrapped in the socks I supplied her with twice a year.

I told her last night that we needed to raid the graveyard behind our house. After a dull day at the office, energy was sucked out of me and I did not have the strength. But she could have done it on her own accord. As long as it served me, I had no objections to her doing stuff. Had she woken me up to a full ashtray, I may have woken her up with my cock in her throat as a reward.

It was the semi-fresh corpses that held the best toenails. I was sure to describe this to her in detail. On this occasion, she refused to take my hints and point-blankly told me that she would not aide me. I did not want her to aide me; I wanted her to go out on her own and dig up bodies.

'There was no babysitter' she cried, ignoring my hints about my total lack of energy. It was true, but the little snot nose brats would be okay for a few hours while they slept if I had the strength to join her and point in the direction of the fleshiest corpses with worms squirming out of their ears. They would never even know they were left alone in the dark. Prior to her recent maternity leave, I left them every night she was out of town on her intense, work-enforced training programmes. I did not like this recent boldness she was displaying. The health visitors fault entirely for encouraging her to attend Mum and Baby groups at the local library. And I would not be going! I did not know what part of my hints and manipulation she failed to understand.

~MY DARLING WIFE~

The shakes hit me before I even switched the alarm to the snooze function. Withdrawal would not allow me the pleasures a snooze offered. It has not done for many years now. There was a time when toenails were plentiful and I could swallow one down while pressing the button for eight more minutes of blissful sleep.

Clamminess washed over me. There was no way I would be able to make it to work like this. I needed toenails to start my morning right. In the grips of withdrawal I could not think of anything other than toenails and scoring toenails. Toenails were all that mattered.

Ripping the duvet away from the wife was the difficult part. She held it in death's grip beneath her chin and tucked between her legs. I became used to never having any blanket – not even a little patch. I would crank up the heat when I woke with my midnight toenail cravings regardless of the season; a little bit of spite courtesy of good ol' dad. My wife would still be reluctant to liberate the duvet despite sleeping in a pool of her own sweat that turned the flakes of dead skin into slush. I once tried to satisfy my cravings with this skin slush; day-long diarrhoea left me on the toilet and the family had to use the outdoor one.

Shaking, it was more difficult to pry the duvet away from her. The withdrawals became worse each day. It seemed her grip on the duvet became tighter as the withdrawals became worse - her subconscious conspiring against me. The back of her mind knew I was no good for her and should trade her in for a younger model.

I only needed access to her feet. Toe jam wasn't as good a substitute for toenails as dick cheese but I needed to make it into work today and every other day for the rest of the fucking year. The board of directors were the biggest bunch of loser arse-ferrets this world has ever seen. I could not even provide an accurate description of what it was I did all day or a clear title for the job that would be on the line if I had a sick day.

TWO

I slid off the bed to the barren floorboards and pulled myself along. It was a ritual I repeated every morning as of late. If my wife wasn't so fucking stupid she would have understood my hints and filled my ashtray while I was gripped in a nightmare world where people were born without toes.

She was forced to sleep wearing microfiber socks and her wet feet coated in Vaseline every night to lock the moisture in. It was the best I could do given my limited resources and inability to think until toenails flowed like a waterfall. Even just a little lick between the toes would starve off the shakes long enough to break into the neighbour's bedroom with my nail clippers. There must be some way I can induce my penis to produce dick cheese for these early morning wake up calls.

The world pressed in. Everything tried to stop me from reaching the toe jam. Even the little splinters on the barren floorboards conspired against me and my addiction. Her feet; so far away they might as well have been located in Lapland dancing with Santa's reindeer. The situation lacked any hope of fulfilment, yet I pulled myself along the floor, taking splinters to my stomach when my silk pyjama top rode up and the matching bottoms rode down.

The stupid bitch I married failed to notice my weight loss (toenails were becoming scarce, I could not eat a normal meal without first nibbling on a toenail or three). She should have noticed and purchased me new pyjamas weeks ago. It only made my hate for her stronger. Hate and resentment were two emotions to make it through the shaking cloud of withdrawal. They came out stronger on the other side.

She farted; a smell that could gas us both, somehow escaping through the fifteen TOG duvet, descended upon me like a million annoying nit-picking scorpions intent on stinging me to death but lacking enough venom to do it. My progress seemed lost in the gas but that was all in my head, the result of the withdrawal I woke up with (it became more intense every day).

I pulled myself along by the forearms – my pyjama bottoms found home around my ankles. Shaking them free would require a different sort of movement, one I could not muster the energy to do while hugged tight in the chocking grip of withdrawal.

If it weren't for the toxic gas leaking from her anus, I would be able to smell the toe jam. Just a few more pulls and I'll have my lips wrapped around her big toe, tonguing between them and licking all the sour goodness. The smell of her feet would keep my motivation high. The chances of her toxic arse gas evaporating were slim to none – there was nowhere for it to go.

My thoughts were not coming in clear – a consequence of inhaling her toxic arse gas and not my own withdrawal. I could always think of toenails and toe jam with utmost clarity when in the grip of withdrawal. Anything to do with toes while in the heights of withdrawal would bring enough comfort and clear thought to score my next hit. But not while my wife's arse was leaking.

Dick cheese spread on toast had a similar impact but not the same as toenails. It was something I had to purchase from drug users in dark alleys. Work has kept me late for the past month, meaning I missed the junkies each night on the way home.

Toxic arse gas was something my body never built up resistance to. Twenty plus years of marriage and I still could not figure out what made her fart and subsequently ban her consumption of it. A blizzard of dust and splinters blew into my face, kicked up by her gas. Withdrawal made my eyes stick out – it would be impossible to close my lids against the assault.

The pain would be there until I wrapped my lips around her toes and sucked away the toe jam and mould lurking there. It hurt to breathe. Each inhale past my shaking lungs was like bringing in microscopic glass shards into my body – tiny sharp edges made me bleed. It was all part of the morning ritual.

Low to the floor, one would be lead to believe I would remain unaffected by her toxic arse gas. The concept was all lies! Once it rose and had no more ceiling to press against, it would have to fill up other spaces in the room. I knew double glazing was a bad idea. The windows sealed the box that was my house and made it airtight to save energy. I was taken in by the sales rep and the pitch she gave as I imagined her on her knees sucking me off immediately following a complete toenail extraction.

Just another six inches and I could pull myself back onto the bed and taste my wife's festering feet. One more pull of my body lagging behind my forearms (limp and dead weight – shaking made it more so) should do it. Breathlessness overcame me by the time I was there. At least less toxic arse gas entered my lungs.

To rest would mean to allow myself to be overcome by the shakes. I needed a nibble before the vomiting and explosive diarrhoea hit. One nibble was all the preventive medicine my body required.

I had been here many times before – every single morning for the past two months, since toenails had started to become scarce. I could not take it much longer. There was no logical reason to explain the recent toenail scarcity. They simply were not growing as fast as they used to, yet my craving remained the same.

I pulled myself back to the bed. Her feet weren't wrapped in the duvet. Their odour could not overpower the scent of her farts. There was not a smell known to man capable of doing that.

The first sock seemed stuck, as it did every morning. They were hard to grasp with the shakes. By the time I had my tongue between her toes, I would forget my intention to buy her Velcro to sew to her crusty socks and myself a pair of gloves with Velcro sewn to the finger tips. Pulling them off would become easier – provided her foot bacteria did not cling on too tight. Walking past Velcro in the supermarket would not remind me of my intentions as long as I had a recent hit of toenails. It was not likely I would go into one of those places without one – the bright overhead lights and crying children hurt my head.

My wife was forbidden to bathe her feet. Mould would grow over night to satisfy my cravings in the morning. I wished for her toenails to grow as fast. No matter how many tablets I ordered online promising rapid nail growth and forced her to swallow, they never seemed to grow quickly enough.

I chanced a nibble. Flesh beneath the mould greeted my teeth. There weren't even cuticles to eat. Toe jam would keep me going through the morning. It would have to. The need to source a fresh supply of toenails was strong. I must sort it out tonight while the world lay in dreamland.

End Excerpt.

ABOUT THE AUTHOR

DANI BROWN is also the author of "Toenails" and "Middle Age Rae of Fucking Sunshine" (both out now from MorbidbookS). When she isn't writing she enjoys knitting and thinking of the finer points of invading Finland with an army of chavs mounted on dingoes. She has an unhealthy obsession with Mayhem's drummer and doesn't trust anyone who claims Velvet Underground as their favourite band.

A DIRTY SHAMEFUL DEVIL OF A SECRET...

Something that two men share. A legacy that will shock you to your very core. One that is created not out of madness, but of the purest desire. Take a vivid journey into the mind of the killer and his biggest fan. Do you believe in evil? See the knife plunge. Lap at the wounds. Do you still? There is no rational meaning or pretty words that will hide away the darkness that the words of this found journal creates. Inside is the real truth.

And it can set you free. Watch all you want. Taste what you dare not have. But once you see, you are in collusion. Keep reading and the guilt will stain. No longer can you feign innocence. The change is as permanent as it is wretched. Perhaps you should just walk away. This shit right here is a MorbidbookS blunt. You dig?

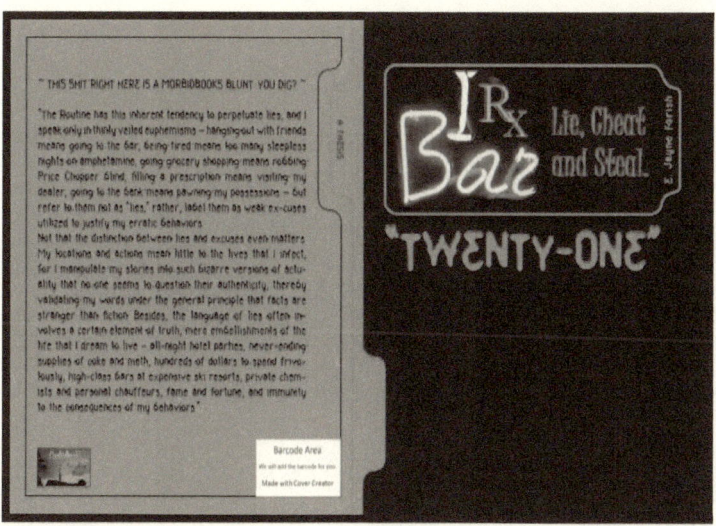

"The Routine has this inherent tendency to perpetuate lies, and I speak only in thinly veiled euphemisms — hanging out with friends means going to the bar; being tired means too many sleepless nights on amphetamine; going grocery shopping means robbing Price Chopper blind; filling a prescription means visiting my dealer; going to the bank means pawning my possessions — but refer to them not as "lies;" rather, label them as weak ex-cuses utilized to justify my erratic behaviors. Not that the distinction between lies and excuses even matters. My locations and actions mean little to the lives that I infect, for I manipulate my stories into such bizarre versions of actuality that no one seems to question their authenticity, thereby validating my words under the general principle that facts are stranger than fiction. Besides, the language of lies often involves a certain element of truth, mere embellishments of the life that I dream to live – all-night hotel parties, never-ending supplies of coke and meth, hundreds of dollars to spend frivolously, high-class bars at expensive ski resorts, private chemists and personal chauffeurs, fame and fortune, and immunity to the consequences of my behaviors."

HUMANITY IS THE DEVIL IS A DECONSTRUCTED

NIGHTMARE mixing David Lynch and snuff movies. The plot revolves around a central character, Seth, who is set about a crusade against humanity which, for him, represents pure evil. Through random killings he and his cronies try to accelerate the end of the world, in order to provoke and defeat the Demiurge, the false God that is ruling the earth. As in Burroughs, logical language is replaced here with cut-scenes – sometimes to be taken literally – that plunge the reader into an extreme experience. Both incredibly morbid and enthralling, HITD is a masterpiece of moral darkness and

existentialist reflection upon our comfortable religion and
morals.

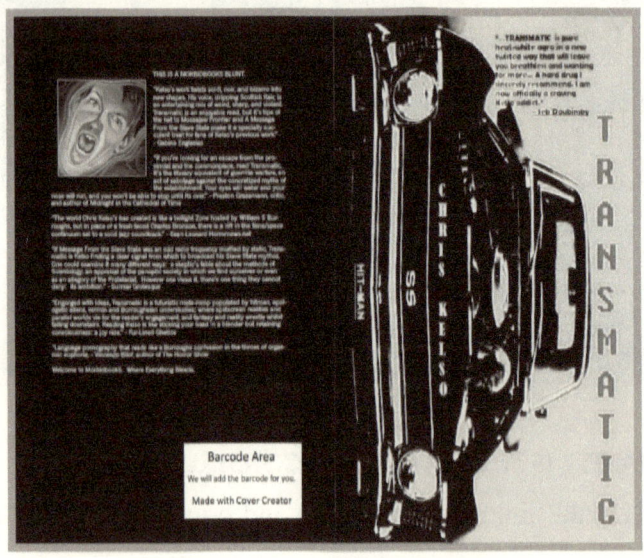

"AS A PART-TIME HITMAN/ EXTERMINATOR, Ignius Ellis's
dream is to buy a candy-apple red Nova Supreme. In the
process of trying to earn enough cash to make his dream
come true he gets sucked into the rough world of Visitacion
Valley, SF. When the tenants in his apartment complex reveal
their various extracurricular activities this take an even more
bizarre twist and Ellis soon becomes acquainted with the
nightmarish Slave State dimension..."

THAT'S THE LAST TIME SHE GETS THE BIGGER WORM...

Once their flesh flakes away the angels collapse into puddles of hissing goop and withered petals blow into them hurried along by unseen winds. My spit looses its sweet taste to the black flavor of ash. The glowing birds in the bright orange sky burst into small sparkly novas. The sky itself weeps and tears, streaking down like a ruined painting as the dismal gray of life wheezes back before my eyes. I don't blink; praying silently for one last desperate sensation of the high. Lila feels it too. She writhes on the mattress next to me; her moans of ecstasy warping into groans that capture the hollowness of our souls. Tears form in her eyes and I can almost feel the lump in her throat. It's gone and she wants to cry. I'd rather chase down more Worms than cry about it but everybody reacts to the Worms differently. I slip away to my own neon colored utopia where things with wings fan me and comfort me when the living neon worm dissolves under my skin. Lila told me once they wrap around her like a giant fuzzy neon hug. I imagine her high shedding off her like snake skin and flaking to the filthy floor next to the mattress. Her high sounds better than mine. More Fun. That's the last time she gets the bigger worm.

~Danielle Brown~

"IF YOU KNOW WHAT KINBAKU, POST-IMPRESSIONISM, and brilliant green eyes have in common, then you are probably a fan of Alex S. Johnson! Congrats! But if you don't know, allow me to open the door, guide you inside, and introduce you to a little Wicked Candy. This is a sweet designed for the discerning Bizarro fan's tastes, and I promise, you will not be disappointed!"

--Mimi Williams, author of Beautiful Monster

"A short collection that both traverses the genre lines and melds them together into one masterpiece. Jam packed with horror, laughs, pop culture history and more, this one is a must have for lovers of the macabre, the bizarre and the hilarious."

--Jeff O'Brien, author of Bigboobenstein

IN GARRETT COOK'S MURDERLAND serial killers are idolized by society. Their deeds are followed obsessively by television pundits and the adoring public. A subculture has grown up around this phenomena, called "Reap." Laws are created to allow this activity to flourish, including designated "safe zones' where killers can practice their trade without fear of persecution. Fans of the top rated serial killers celebrate each new kill on social media and television. Programs glorify their deeds.

The culture of Murderland is violent and mirrors our own violent society and its decadent obsessions; but Murderland isn't about how violent the world has become. It's about the pervasive nature of media and how it corrupts. It corrupts absolutely.

At the heart of Murderland is Jeremy Jenkins. Jeremy doesn't like what he sees and he's just enough insane to believe he can do something about it, that he can change the world. His methods are extreme- to outdo the serial killers, he'll kill THEM, turn their own twisted reality back on themselves. It's a hopeless task, impossible, Herculean; but it's Jeremy's fate to see it through to the end.

The three sections of Murderland comprise a true Homeric epic. In the first section we are shown the terrible world Jeremy lives in, the world that if we look at it honestly, is really our own world. We meet all the principal characters, the serial killers, the pundits, the pawns, and Jeremy's beloved Cass. In the second section Jeremy goes on a bit of a spiritual quest and comes to understand his true purpose. In the final section the flames are ignited and all hell breaks loose. Jeremy, like a great epic hero must journey to the underworld and be reborn in order to triumph.

BORN WHOLE FROM THE RECTUM of a dying patient, Morbid silently stalks the hospital's hallways, heinously dispatching the most helpless of patients and in the most painfully repulsive of manners. In the meantime, in order to pay for his family and home that includes his ghost step-father Sammy and his pet aborted fetus Chip, Westphal has to ingest mounds of dangerous narcotics to get through his night shifts. Barely hanging on to his Care Tech gig by his fingernails, the last thing Westphal needs is to be accused of Morbid's evil deeds. You, on the other hand, simply want to find some solace. Terminally ill from a virulent infection, and dependent on Life Support, all You beg for a peaceful and dignified demise. Shirk has other plans for You. The ancient drug-snuffling demon makes You relive all of your deadly and venial sins as he tortures You. Night after night. Until eternal Damnation begins for YOU MORBID WESTPHAL, yet again.... NOW WITH EVEN *MORE* EVIL FLAVOR!

IT LOOKS LIKE CAROLYN AND MARK

are in deep, deep shit...

Mark and Carolyn live in an alternate 1989 where Ronald Reagan is on his fourth presidential term. The USA has a rigid, long-standing caste system and abortions were never made legal. Being homeless is a crime that is punishable by imprisonment in an internment camp the inmates call Tent City. Most of Mark's ER patients are inmates at this camp and are victims of a new disease these illegals call the Transient Flu. This deadly and rapidly spreading disease mutates with each new host, collecting information, changing code. The disease evolves lightning quick, spreading like pond ripples and infecting everyone. No one is safe. Mark and Carolyn dig too deep and uncover the brutal truth: Transient Flu was purposely made and is one hundred percent fatal. Carolyn's employer, Hudson-Smythe Pharmaceuticals, discovers the chain of evidence. It traces the pharmacide back to Hudson-Smythe and the crime of the century. Cost is no object and deadly force is authorized. Yes. Carolyn and Mark are in deep, deep shit.

IMMANUEL THE CHRIST HAS SOME NERVE. Jonah has

already lost everyone he loves to Pilate the vampire and his

Harbor drug violence. Jonah now trudges through his days

staying as high on Plata as possible. He just wants to be left

alone while he waits for his turn to die. The Christ has other

plans for him. She sends Her messenger, Pedro, to assign

Jonah the very dangerous task of ordering the Herod to

dismantle the Harbor's Plata trade. Jonah decides to run. But

you can't run from God forever. As Jonah learns the hard way

when the 'Edmund Fitzgerald' founders and goes down in

rough seas, with the reluctant prophet on board. Job is Satan's

Chosen One and he doesn't take kindly to orders from some upstart prophet.

'click' on banner for more Kindle books from MbS!